D1525636

# Rory: A Scottish Outlaw

**Highland Outlaws, Volume 3**

Lily Baldwin

Published by Lily Baldwin, 2021.

RORY: A SCOTTISH OUTLAW

**First edition. March 13, 2021.**

Written by Lily Baldwin.

To McKenzie

I'll meet you under the rainbow.

# Chapter One
# Scotland
# 1302

Rory MacVie's horse nickered and tossed its head. "Hush, lass," he crooned, leaning forward to stroke her thick, black mane.

"He should be here already," David hissed. "I don't like this."

Rory glanced sidelong at his agitated friend before once more scanning the surrounding woods, still illuminated by summer's twilight. "Give him time," Rory said. "Ye're always too quick to worry."

Several moments passed in silence. Then Rory rolled his eyes at David who had grabbed up his reins.

"Something's not right," David growled. "Let's go."

"Ye need to calm down," Rory began, but then he heard a branch snap deep in the thicket. "Wait," he hissed, grabbing David's forearm, stopping him from turning his horse about. "Listen."

Leaves rustled the instant before a flash of movement through the trees caught Rory's eye. "He's coming," Rory whispered.

A white horse nosed its way into the clearing, carrying a cloaked figure. Rory's eyes narrowed, taking in the person's diminutive stature. They had expected a man, not a mere lad.

He flexed his hand, ready to grab the sword strapped to his back if need be as he watched the rider turn his horse to face them, stopping several paces away. Rory tensed when a small hand peeked out from beneath the voluminous folds of black cloak and pulled back the draping hood.

"Bloody hell," Rory cursed under his breath as he locked eyes with an intensely beautiful woman. Flaxen hair shone nearly as white as her snowy skin.

A slow smile curved her lips before she dipped her head and said, "*Alba gu bràth*." Scotland forever.

"*Alba gu bràth*," Rory said, repeating the secret password of their cause.

"Who the hell are ye?" David growled, his harsh tone causing Rory to wince.

"Don't be an arse," Rory snapped before turning apologetically back to the woman in front of them. "Forgive my friend, but we were supposed to be meeting one Alex MacKenzie."

"And so ye have," she replied, her lips now stretching into a full smile—lips so luscious Rory could almost taste their sweetness in his mouth. "I am Alex MacKenzie," she said.

The sharp scraping of a blade leaving its sheath drew Rory's attention away from the distracting image.

"What are ye doing?" he asked, shaking his head in disapproval as David pointed his sword at the lass.

"She's a trap," David snapped. "The English must have taken the real Alex and are baiting us with a pretty skirt."

An indignant harrumph drew Rory's gaze back to the woman.

Her eyes flashed bright with anger. "I am, indeed, Alex MacKenzie."

God's blood but he loved a spirited lass.

"Aye, then prove it," David taunted. "Where's the coin. Ye've no satchel, chests or saddlebags. If ye're Alex MacKenzie, then where's Scotland's money?"

She cocked a golden brow before slowly sliding from her horse and landing on the ground with a heavy thud. "Ye spook easily," she said to David.

Rory chuckled. "Ye don't know the half of it."

Once more, she locked eyes with him. "I require yer assistance."

He needed no urging. In fact, he could think of nothing more he wanted to do in that moment than assist a beautiful Scottish rebel.

"Don't trust her," David hissed.

Rory hesitated. Could David be right? Could he be walking into a trap?

Alex raised her brow at him. "Are ye as skittish as yer friend?"

That settled matters. Rory never backed down from a challenge, especially when issued from lips as exquisitely shaped as hers. How could he resist? He slid from his horse and walked toward her, but then she turned her back on him. Confusion stopped him in his tracks. He glanced back at David, but his friend only lifted his shoulders, clearly equally as baffled.

Rory turned around in time to watch her cloak drop to the ground. "My laces, if ye please," she said.

He stared at her long, slender back for a moment, contemplating what to do. Just as he made it a point never to back away from a challenge, he also never said no to that particular request. Still, a strange woman asking him to untie her laces in the middle of a vast forest with another man looking on was a first. He cleared his throat and closed the distance between them. Who was he to deny any lass such a simple favor? His fingers worked quickly, and in a flash, her surcote dropped to a heap around her ankles. Then she bent in front of him, giving him a stunning view of her round derriere as she grabbed the hem of her tunic. Standing, she began pulling off the dark green wool.

"If ye please," she said sharply. The fabric around her head muffled her voice but did nothing to shield him from her annoyance.

He grabbed hold of her tunic and whisked it off her raised arms.

"I should have asked yer friend to help," she said, glancing up at him. "Perhaps he has more practice undressing women."

Another challenge.

Rory stepped forward, his eyes scanning the length of her. "In the future, when I remove yer clothes, I promise not to tarry."

"Then show me ye're a man of yer word. There are layers to go still." She flashed him a smile before bending to grab the hem of her second tunic.

He swallowed the groan that rushed up his throat as he grasped the fabric from her hands and began to lift the dress, but he was amazed by its weight.

"Why the hell is this so heavy?" Rory asked.

"Did the prospect of seeing me naked somehow make ye forget why we're here?" she crooned, her voice low and seductive.

"The coin?" Rory said.

She nodded.

He eased the laden fabric over her head, revealing her kirtle. The thin fabric pressed taut against her full breasts and hugged her shapely curves.

His mouth watered when she bent at the waist, lifting the hem of her under-dress.

"Ye can't be hiding anymore?" Rory said, tightly clutching the heavy tunic.

She grinned playfully and lifted her kirtle higher, exposing a slender dirk strapped to her thigh. The blade glinted when she eased it from its sheath. Then she dropped her kirtle in place and reached for the tunic he held. She flipped back a portion. Straightaway, he noticed the small square patches sewn into the interior. She pricked at the fabric with the tip of her dirk, catching one of the patches and slicing it open, exposing a silver mark. "The entire dress is lined in them—from the bottom hem to the neckline, even down the sleeves. 'Tis a small fortune in silver."

"However did ye manage to mount yer horse in this thing?" he asked.

"I had a boost," she said coyly. "I will of course require yer assistance once more," she said, pointing to her garments still in a heap on the ground.

Setting the coin-filled garment down, he reached for the other tunic. After pulling it down over her head, he smoothed the fabric in place, running his hand down the gentle curve where her slim waist flared to her rounded hip.

"Ye have strong hands," she said softly over her shoulder to him.

Her praise fueled his ardor. Resisting the desire to tear off the very tunic he had just fitted into place, he grabbed her rumpled surcote and began easing the thick worsted wool over her head. Tying the laces, his eyes drank their fill, memorizing the lines of her narrow waist and rich curves.

She whirled around, surprising him the instant after he cinched the final knot. They locked eyes. Then her gaze dropped, journeying over his person with the same slow and sensual deliberation he had shown her lovely form.

When her eyes once again met his, she released a long breath before saying, "Regretfully, I must go."

He stepped closer. "Will we meet again?"

Giving no answer, she reached for the reins of her horse. "A leg up please?"

He stepped closer and laced his fingers together. She put a knee in his hands, and he lifted as she pulled herself up and into the saddle with practiced ease.

His left hand lingered on her knee for a moment. He looked up at her, the intensity of her gaze fueling his desire to greater heights. "Will we meet again?" he said, repeating his question.

She lifted one of her shoulders. "Who can say what the future holds?"

Rory clenched his fist to keep from pulling her back off the horse and into his arms. "I hope my future holds ye," he said, his voice low and husky. "It would be a tragedy were I never to taste those lips."

She flashed him a smile. "Ye're in luck." She leaned over in the saddle, grabbed his tunic and pressed her full lips hard against his. Desire quickly overcame his initial surprise. He reached his hand around the back of her neck and deepened their kiss. A soft groan escaped her when she drew away. "Thank ye," she whispered.

"For what?" he breathed through a haze of shock and desire.

She smiled. "For being a loyal servant to Scotland." Then she drove her heel into her horse's flank and sped off down the forest road.

He stared after her. The sweetness of her kiss lingered in his mouth, never to be forgotten, even as she disappeared into the fading light.

# Chapter Two

Rory sat at his usual corner table in the Sunk Ship, a bawdy tavern in the seaside village of Gaillean. Raucous laughter from fishermen, unwinding after a long day at sea, competed with the lyrical voices of barmaids and prostitutes, the latter vying for the attention of the wealthiest, youngest, or handsomest clientele. Painted lips and charcoal-lined eyes flashed in Rory's direction, but the scowl that furrowed his brow kept the lassies at bay. He lifted a tankard of ale to his lips, took a slow sip and scanned the room.

A man named Tamhas with thinning gray hair and a bushy beard raised his mug in greeting when Rory caught his eye. Tamhas was the proprietor of the Sunk Ship and possessed a loquacious tongue, but Rory was in no mood for conversation. On a different night, he might have called Tamhas over; instead, Rory only nodded in greeting, then immediately looked away and eased back in his seat. Resting his head against the cool stones behind him, he stared up at the iron candelabra dangling from the ceiling while he worked to shut out the surrounding frivolity.

"Rory!"

He jolted upright and looked at the man sitting across the table.

David slammed his mug down. "Finally, I have yer attention."

Rory's scowl deepened. "I'm right here. Ye don't need to shout or break Tamhas's table."

"Really? Because I'm not so sure about that. I've said yer name a half a dozen times, and ye've only just noticed. What the bloody hell is wrong with ye?"

Rory shrugged. "Ye have my attention now," he said dryly, ignoring his friend's question.

David's shoulder-length blond hair fell in front of his hard, green eyes as he leaned over the table and hissed in a low voice, "I'm trying to talk to ye about what the abbot said at our last meeting. Remember?" He raked his hand through his hair, uncovering his eyes, which narrowed on Rory. "While a truce is in place between Scotland and England, we're supposed to rally the people. We're supposed to be turning farmers into soldiers."

Rory motioned for David to stop speaking as a barmaid sauntered up to the table holding a tray of brimming tankards. She bent at the waist, giving Rory a view of her smooth, full bosom, which loomed above her cinched bodice. Strawberry ringlets dripped from her temples, framing her heart-shaped face.

Rory fingered one of the curls and swept a slow gaze across her creamy skin, but her overt display did little to stir his desire. His body throbbed with need, but no one in that room could satisfy his hunger. Only one woman had that power—one with the heart of a Scottish rebel.

Rory shifted his eyes, looking down at his fresh tankard of ale. "Thank ye," he muttered.

"For the love of God, man, what ails ye?"

Rory looked at David in surprise. "If I cared, I would ask the same question of ye."

Another woman sauntered by just then, her hips swinging in a sensual rhythm. Rory recognized her as one of the lassies who worked upstairs. He followed the movement of her hips for a moment longer before looking back down at the golden liquid in his cup, which he found to be the most appealing thing in the room.

David threw his hands up, once more drawing Rory's gaze. "Bloody hell, Rory. As usual, ye've got every woman in this room throwing herself at ye, and ye're not taking even one kiss, one nibble."

Rory shrugged. "I see nothing that catches my fancy."

David rolled his eyes. "Don't even try to tell me that strawberry tart over there with all the curves escaped yer notice. I've known ye a long time. She's exactly the type to catch yer fancy."

Rory glanced once more at the red-haired lass who now sat on Tamhas's lap but kept her eyes trained on him. David was right. Normally, her round bottom would be pressed against his lap. Her luscious breasts bobbing up and down close to his hungry lips. But tonight, he had no interest.

David leaned close. "What occupies yer mind so?"

Rory absently trailed his finger around the brim of his cup. "I was just wondering how long it took Alex to sew all those coins into her tunic."

"Ah-ha," David exclaimed, jumping to his feet, the scrape of his chair drawing the surrounding revelers' gazes. "That chit? That's what this is all about?"

It was Rory's turn to roll his eyes. "Sit down, would ye?"

David eased back down, shaking his head. "Ye've got yer head in the clouds over a lass." He leaned forward. "I'm trying to talk ye about rallying the people, building armies, taking back our country, putting a bloody Scottish king on the bloody thrown while ye're daydreaming about some bleeding lass."

David stood and turned around, gesturing across the room. "A little strawberry tart will make ye forget Alex MacKenzie for good."

Rory leaned to look past David at the 'strawberry tart' whose pretty face suddenly lit up with a wide smile. "Damnation," he cursed and grabbed David's hand out of the air, flattening it on the table. "What the hell do ye think ye're doing?"

"I'm getting ye a warm and willing lass to share yer bed so ye can get yer head back to business."

"I have not needed help filling my bed since I shaved my first whiskers. I already told ye—I'm not interested."

David crossed his arms over his chest. "Yer lack of interest is the bleeding point. Fine. Have it yer way. Deny yerself a warm bed. That is yer own choice to make. Pine after some lass ye may never see again—also yer choice. But ye cannot allow this infatuation to distract ye from what's important. The cause is bigger than us both. The pining of yer heart is of no consequence. Ye've made a vow to yer brothers-at-arms and to the abbot. Anyway, do ye think King Edward is sitting idly by with a drink in one hand and a ripe arse in the other? Nay. Ye and I both know this truce will not last. He spends his days bleeding his people dry with taxes to amass more weapons, horses, and soldiers. We must rebuild Scotland's army as he does. Rory, the time to rally the people is now!"

Rory tossed down the rest of his ale and swiped the back of his sleeve across his lips. "Ye want me to rally the people, do ye?" He stood. "I'll rally the people." Cupping his hands around his mouth, he shouted. "We're going to fight for Scottish independence. Who's with us?"

The room erupted into cheers. Chuckling, Rory sat down and winked at David. "Don't fash yerself. Ye know where my loyalties lie."

Just then another barmaid leaned over and thumped down two full tankards, sloshing ale on the table. Rory pressed a kiss to her blushing cheek before raising his cup to David. "*Alba gu bràth*." Scotland Forever.

David sat back in his chair, a rare smile playing at his lips. "*Alba gu bràth*."

Rory set his tankard down and reached toward the wooden tray in the center of the table. He passed over the cheese and bread, choosing a red apple. A fleeting sadness caused a pang in his heart. Apples always reminded him of his wee sister, Roslyn. She was one of thousands of innocents slain on the streets of Berwick when King Edward of England claimed the once Scottish city for himself.

At the time, Rosalyn had been selling apples in Berwick's once bustling marketplace. Six years had passed. The approaching winter would have marked her thirteenth year. His grip tightened around the apple as the all too familiar fury laid claim to his soul. The Berwick massacre had completely altered Rory's life. Once he had worked the docks alongside his da, but both his parents had also been cut down in the streets. He and his four brothers and eldest sister had been forced to flee their demolished city, becoming exiles. That was when Rory first took up the cause, alongside his siblings. His dedication had never wavered, nor would it do so now. His first priority would always be Scotland.

He knew Abbot Matthew was right. The time had come to rally the people. He set the apple down among the bread and cheese and locked eyes with David. "Weapons," he said.

"What the devil are ye talking about now?"

Rory leaned forward. "If Abbot Matthew wishes to turn farmers into soldiers, we'll need weapons."

The door swung open just then drawing Rory's gaze. Into the Sunk Ship walked a scrawny lad. Rory guessed he had no more than ten years to his credit. He kept his eyes down and crossed straight to where the barkeep stood, uncorking a new barrel of ale. The man bent to give the lad his ear. Moments later, again without looking up, the boy dashed out the door. A shiver of expectation shot up Rory's spine when the barkeep turned and looked directly at him and made the sign of the cross.

Rory stood. "Abbot Matthew is looking for me."

David raised his glass. "To another mission. *Alba gu bràth*."

"Indeed," Rory said before setting out across the room.

"Rory!"

Rory glanced back when he heard David's call.

"Maybe he can reveal something about Alex MacKenzie."

Rory smiled. "Why do ye think I'm leaving now and not after I've finished my ale?"

# Chapter Three

M orning sunlight painted the village in soft golden hues and wrapped around Alex like a warm blanket as she wound her way through the narrow village paths. Regrettably, her current mission did not involve smuggling coin or protecting rebel secrets; she was simply making the rounds, checking in on every MacKenzie in the village. Although she was happy to once again be home among her people, she was already feeling restless. She thrived on her secret work for the cause. Still, having been gone from the Highlands for nearly a month, it was her duty as lady of Luthmore Castle to ensure her people's needs were met, and with her wee brother at her side, she was seeing to that—

Alex stopped and looked around. William was nowhere to be seen.

"Will," she called back down the lane. Then a red-haired lad of twelve years, pulling a small cart laden with bread, cloth, and other essentials, came barreling around the corner, a broad smile lighting his freckled face.

"Arabel's wee ones wouldn't let me leave until I'd given them all shoulder rides," Will said, arriving breathless at her side. He rubbed one of his shoulders. "Her oldest, Calum, is only three years younger than me. It was not an easy task."

Alex laughed and resisted the urge to ruffle his hair. "The Lord will bless ye for the joy ye gave them." Her heart swelling with pride, she pulled him close in a warm embrace. Will was not her brother by birth, but she could not have loved him more. He became her wee brother just weeks after he was born when both his parents had succumbed to illness.

Alex remembered that sorrowful day well.

It was the morning after her seventh birthday. Her mother, Alana, who regularly suffered from severe coughing spells, had awoken feeling a little short of breath. Over the course of the morning, the cough settled into her chest and soon she was wheezing and sweating. Alex's father, Donnan, carried Alana to their chamber. Alex followed behind with careful steps, clasping a bowl with the cook's remedy for her mother's breathing attacks, a big scoop of mustard powder, mixed with vinegar and honey. Dipping her head, she smelled the concoction. The pungent fragrance made her eyes water. Once inside her parent's chamber, her father laid her mother down. Still, she wheezed and sputtered for breath.

"I'll take that now, Alex," one of her mother's maids said. "I'll make a compress for yer mum's chest, and she'll feel better in no time."

"Come along now, Alex," her father said, drawing her gaze away from her mother's suffering. Donnan scooped her into his arms. His gentle smile soothed her worry. "She'll be better soon. Ye'll see." Then he glanced back at Alana. Alex did not miss the fleeting look of concern that pinched his features before he gave her a toss in the air and threw her over his shoulder like a sack of potatoes. "Come along, my sweet lass. We've work to do in the village."

The sun had risen high in the sky, and Alex and her father were still making the rounds when the village midwife, Morag, came rushing at them, hollering for her laird.

"Ye must come, Donnan," she cried. "Thomas and Rhona, the poor lambs, have taken a turn for the worse. 'Tis grave. There isn't a moment to lose. I'm on my way to fetch Father John."

Alex and her father hurried to the cottage of a young couple who had been ill for days.

"We were just here, Da," Alex whispered, gripping tighter to his hand. "Remember? A few weeks ago, we came to welcome their baby into the clan."

Brows drawn, her father knelt in front of her. "I remember, pet. Now, listen. Wait out here for me. No matter what happens, do not come inside. Ye ken?"

Her heart suddenly felt heavy in her chest. Despite her tender years, she knew something truly dreadful was happening. She nodded in reply, unable to speak for the knot that had gathered in her throat.

"Good lass," her father said. Then he pressed a hurried kiss to her forehead the instant before he turned and disappeared inside the cottage.

Within minutes of Donnan's arrival, Father John hurried down the lane and went into the cottage. He had been there no time at all before stepping back out.

"Father, what's wrong?" Alex asked.

He looked up as if only just noticing her there. "Ah, my lady, Thomas has left this earthly life. We can only pray for his soul now."

Alex remembered well when other clansmen arrived to remove Thomas's shrouded body to the church, followed by a wake of anguished villagers. Not knowing what else to do, she'd followed them.

*"Tis such a tragedy. They were so very young."*

*"Aye. He died as soon as the laird arrived, as if he'd been waiting for another man to take his place."*

*"Little good it will do. Rhona is not long for this world either."*

*"And the poor wee bairn. What's to become of him?"*

After a few moments, the mournful procession filled her with fear. Heart racing, she turned away and darted back to the cottage, longing for the protection of her da's embrace. But just before her fingers connected with the slatted wood door, she froze, remembering her promise not to go inside no matter what occurred. Taking a deep breath, her trembling fingers pushed the door open—only a crack—not enough to see inside, just enough to hear Rhona's dying pleas and rattled breaths and Donnan's words of comfort.

"Take my son," Rhona pleaded. "Make him yers, Donnan. 'Tis the only way...to save him from the doom that has marked his new life."

Her father's warm voice reached Alex's ears. "Yer son will want for nothing. I promise ye."

"Nay," Rhona cried, her voice straining against fatigue and pain. "I ken...ye'll care for him. I'm asking ye to make him yers—not yer heir...just yer son... Give him yer heart."

Alex peered around the door then, despite her father's command to remain outside and away from the tainted air. Women knelt along one side of the dying lass's pallet, sobbing, while Donnan knelt on her other side. Alex watched as her father took Rhona's trembling hands in his own strong calloused ones. "I promise ye, I will. Yer son will be invited into my heart and my home. I will love him as if he were my own. He shall grow to valor. He will come to believe in his own worth, and above all, I will teach him kindness—the true mark of any man."

Peace fell over Rhona's face, softening away the pain that had marred her youthful beauty. "Thank ye," she said in a whisper that barely reached Alex's ears. Her father leaned over and pressed a kiss to Rhona's forehead. Then he continued to sit with her, cradling her hands in his, whispering soothing words that Alex could not hear, but she could feel the warmth and peace they held.

"Aunt Alana is feeling a little better."

Alex's head jerked up. Her cousin, Mary, younger by two years, looked down at her, her little brows drawn together. Mary knelt beside Alex. "What has happened? Everyone is whispering and crying."

"Thomas died," Alex said, her voice breaking. "Rhona is going to die, too."

Tears flooded Mary's eyes. "But then their new baby won't have a mum or da, like me."

Alex swallowed the thick knot in her throat and nodded.

"But who will he live with?" Mary cried. "When my parents died, I came to Luthmore. Where will the baby have to go?"

Alex wrapped her arm around Mary. "I'm not certain, but I think he is going to live with us."

Long after the sun had set and candles illuminated the small cottage, William's young mother slipped from their world with the laird of the MacKenzie at her side. When her body was taken to the kirk to rest beside Thomas, Alex's father took William from the woman who had been tending him. He turned to where Alex and Mary sat together, their backs against the side of the cottage.

Tears streaming down his cheeks, Donnan knelt and showed the girls William's sweet face. "Alex and Mary, this is yer new brother. He is ours now. Take him into yer hearts and love him always."

Remembering that day never failed to pain Alex's heart, but the memories also served to inspire her. For it was on that day she realized the kind of man her father was, and now, at nineteen, she was old enough to have learned that not enough men were like Donnan MacKenzie.

To her father, being chieftain was not a right of birth; it was a privilege, a call to serve. The clansmen and women who looked to him as leader also saw a friend, a parent, someone they could lean on during times that tried the soul. He also ensured that all levels of leadership within the clan held tightly to the same principles whether steward, captain of the guard, or stable master. What's more, binding himself to a woman who embodied these same ideals had been paramount in his selection of a wife, and he had found his match in Alana.

Alex used to strive to be exactly like her mother, but as she grew, she realized that no one could ever be as kind, compassionate, and as refined as Alana. Unlike her mother, Alex was often rash, sharp-tongued, easily distracted, and incapable of yielding to the demands of convention, especially when there was so much work to be done. But her mother seldom scolded her for going about barefoot or wearing worn-out tunics. Kindness mattered most to Alana, a truth she had instilled in Alex. And before Alana passed away from her illness during her daughter's thirteenth summer, she had made certain Alex understood that the wellbeing of the people came first.

Her father had struggled with his grief for several years. Donnan and Alana had loved each other dearly and had hoped Alex might know the same happiness in marriage. The thought made Alex sigh out loud. How would she find a husband worthy of her clan's chiefdom?

A new wave of sadness gripped her heart as she started off down the lane, this time helping Will pull the wagon to give his shoulder a rest. There had been a time when she believed she had found a worthy man. When she was fifteen her father had betrothed her to one of his closest and most trusted friends, Lord Robin Campbell, who had possessed holdings several leagues south of MacKenzie territory. Although Robin had been more than twenty years her senior, she had supported her father's choice from the start. Robin was a man of honor, conviction, and kindness—a truly great man like her father. But like her father, Robin had been unable to sit idly by and watch Scotland fall to its knees in front of an English king, and so he had taken up the cause. He put blacksmiths to work making weapons. He ran messages and collected funds. And he fought alongside her father, raising his sword high for Scotland at the battle of Dunbar. Despite honor being on their side, the Scots were defeated. Her father returned from war on the brink of death with injuries from which he would never fully recover, while Robin did not return at all.

"Welcome home, Alex," a raspy voice called out, thankfully releasing Alex's thoughts from the mire of despair.

Shaking off the past, she jogged over to where an old man sat carving a piece of wood. "Good morrow, Corc. How do ye fare?"

Corc rubbed his knobby knees, which peeked out beneath his plaid. "My old bones do a lot of talking these days, but I choose to ignore them. They never have anything interesting to say."

Alex smiled and reached down to squeeze the old man's gnarled fingers. "Yer a brave man, Corc, but if ye're uncomfortable, have Morag make ye up a tisane to sip in the evening."

He waved his hand dismissively. "I don't want to be any trouble."

Alex cocked a brow at him. "Ye know ye wouldn't be any trouble. Anyway, Morag's always good for a laugh, and ye know how she enjoys gossiping."

Corc smiled, revealing the few teeth he still had left. "Aye, true enough—and then I'd have an excuse to see her other than my aches and pains. I can claim it's all a ruse to find some decent conversation—no shame in that."

Alex chuckled. "None at all." Then she turned to Will. "Bring along some bread for Corc."

Corc waved Will away. "Nay, the lassies here in the village keep me fat as butter. Give that to someone else."

Alex took the loaf from her brother's hand and thrust it at Corc. "It makes me happy. Accept it as a favor to me."

Corc's face softened. Then he flashed his wide, gummy smile. "Ye know I can't refuse now."

"Oh, I know," Alex said, winking.

Corc wrapped his weathered fingers around the loaf. "Thank ye, Alex. Ye're a fine lass. Yer mother would be proud.

We all missed ye while ye were away. But I think it right good of ye to visit Haddington in your father's stead. Knowing yer father as I do, he values the time ye spend with the abbot, although I ken it must be dull for ye, cooped up praying with all those monks. The silence alone would kill me."

Alex suppressed the smile Corc's words prompted as flashes of her last 'visit' to Haddington Abbey came unbidden to her mind. Of course, few knew where she had really been. Even her escort to Haddington remained ignorant of her true purpose. Every time she went, the warriors were put to work ploughing Haddington's fields, harvesting crops, repairing outbuildings or doing anything else to help the community. Alex, being the sole woman there, ate and slept in seclusion. Her men were completely unaware that their lady had actually left the monastery altogether.

Likewise, her most trusted adviser, Michael, steward of Luthmore, had no notion that she was an agent for the righteous cause of Scottish independence. Only Mary and her lady's maid, Rosie, knew the truth. As far as the rest of the MacKenzie's were concerned, she traveled to the monastery in her father's stead, bringing his donations and taking the opportunity for prayer and contemplation within its hallowed walls.

And once upon a time this story had been true. But only once.

It was on her first visit to Abbot Matthew that she confessed her desire to take up the cause in Robin's stead, and from that moment on, she and the abbot had been in league together. She smuggled stolen coin, delivered messages, and gathered weapons, just as Robin had done. Her most recent mission had involved a great deal of planning. The abbot had amassed a large amount of silver, which for more than two years had been hidden away within a small kirk in a village in the Highlands. Alex had volunteered to move the coin. It had not taken her long to think of the idea of lining her tunic with the silver; however, it had taken her, Rosie, and Mary an age to sew the individual marks in place. Alex's breath caught. Remembering her coin-lined dress drove her thoughts instantly toward sky-blue eyes; coal-black hair; strong, capable hands; and full lips pressed hard against her own.

"Alex!"

She was jarred from her thoughts as a small body barreled into her. Alex smiled down into the upturned, impish face of a wee lass with tangled red curls and golden-brown eyes. "Good morrow, Cassie."

"We've been waiting for ye over there," the little girl said, raising a chubby arm and pointing at the next cottage farther down the lane.

Alex turned back to Corc. "Apparently, 'tis time for Will and me to move on."

"Go in peace, Alex. I'll pray for yer health and safety and for the health of yer father."

Alex bent at the waist and pressed a kiss to his wizened cheek. Then with a smile and a wave, she started back down the path with Cassie straddling her hip.

"Good morrow, dear friend," Alex said to the woman standing in the cottage doorway with three wee bairns clinging to her skirts.

"'Tis a fine morning now that ye've returned, Alex."

Alex put Cassie down and pulled Helen into a tight embrace. "Oh, I've missed ye."

Helen furrowed her brow with concern. "Are ye well? Ye look a bit flushed."

Alex could not entirely stop the smile that fought to spread her lips wide. "I'm well enough, but I tell ye, Helen," she said, leaning closer and dropping her voice. "I met a man while I was away that could bring any woman to her knees with a single glance."

"Dear me," Helen said, her bright eyes shining with mischief. "Please tell me ye're not speaking of one of the monks at Haddington."

Alex cocked her brow at her friend. "I'm not entirely lacking in scruples."

"I ken," Helen said, laughing. "'Twas a jest. Thankfully, the principles of yer soul hold the rather wanton demands of yer body in check. 'Tis a good thing too, or ye'd have lost yer virtue long ago. So, where did ye meet this man, and when are ye going to marry him and give Luthmore an heir?"

"Nay, not ye, too," Alex groaned. "Ye sound just like Michael." Her father's steward never ceased pestering her about her duties as lady to Luthmore Castle—procuring a husband remained at the very top of his list, that and wearing shoes.

"'Tis high time ye settled down. Anyway, ye need to get yerself a man. He'll help cool those flushed cheeks."

"Ye ken 'tis not a lack of desire to wed on my part, but who can I trust to hold authority over my people? The good men are dead or taken, and the bad ones simply won't get past my gate. Anyway, Da's health is not up to the task right now."

Helen's head tilted slightly to the side as she gave Alex a knowing look. "Is there no one who could capture yer heart?"

"I gave my heart to Robin."

"I'm speaking of love, Alex," Helen insisted, stepping closer. Alex flinched. "Ye know I loved Robin."

"Of course ye did," Helen said, giving her hand a squeeze. "Ye respected him and admired him, and deservedly so. But, Alex, ye were never in love with him. The sight of him never made yer knees weak or stole yer breath. And don't play innocent with me. Since ye lost him, I know ye've been kissed properly."

Alex smiled but lifted her shoulders in defeat. "I'm fairly certain ladies aren't allowed to marry for love."

Helen pointed at Alex's grubby feet. "Nor are they meant to go about barefoot, allowing commoners to use their Christian names, but that's never stopped ye." A slow smiled curved Helen's lips as she studied Alex. "I can tell ye're losing patience with me, so I'll stop nagging. 'Tis just...God forbid something were to happen to yer da. Ye'd be leaving the lot of us without a laird for protection."

An ache coiled around Alex's heart, nigh stealing her breath. What Helen didn't know—what few knew—was how sick her father really was.

Donnan had returned home from the battle of Dunbar alive but forever damaged. An enemy blade had struck his head, knocking off his helmet while another English knight took a swing with a mace, crushing his skull. Rendered unconscious, he fell to the ground where horses trampled his legs, crushing the bones. Only by the grace of God did Donnan survive, but he never walked again nor did his mind fully heal. Memories from before the battle came to him with ease, but when the sun set on a new day, most of his new memories were gone come morning. Also, stolen by the vicious blow to his skull was his ability to read and do sums. With regard to his lasting injuries, the clan only knew half the story. Everyone understood that Donnan would be bedridden for the remainder of his days, but Alex, and those closest to the laird, had concealed the weaknesses of Donnan's mind—an addle-minded chieftain meant a vulnerable clan. And so, at sixteen, Alex took on the role of laird, but her every command remained always in Donnan's name. The rest of their kin, and most importantly, neighboring clans, believed that Donnan's mind was sharp as ever, and that he issued orders from his chamber, which Alex simply ensured were carried out.

Alex slumped down at Helen's table, suddenly weary, and accepted a cup of mead from her friend's outstretched hand. "Thank ye," she said and took a long sip, absently stroking her hand across a piece of soft, dark blue wool folded on the table. "'Tis lovely," Alex said, admiring the fabric closer.

"Aye, 'tis that," Helen agreed. "I bought it from a peddler who came through the village yesterday."

Alex straightened in her seat. "Not the same peddler who came through last spring?"

Helen shook her head. "Of course not—ye know that man would never again get within a league of MacKenzie territory."

Relief eased the sudden tension from Alex's shoulders as she again sat back. More than a year had passed since a dreadful beast of a man swept through town, selling rotted grain, soiled fabrics, and lewd wooden carvings. Alex had only been made aware of his presence after several villagers had come to the keep, complaining of a peddler who was trying to frighten and bully them into buying his objectionable goods. Flanked by two of the largest MacKenzie warriors, Gavin and Finlay, she had marched down and confronted the rodent—a sniveling Englishman, small in stature with greasy black hair, and cold, hard eyes. At first, she cast him from her lands in a firm but calm voice. In reply, he spat on the ground saying, "I don't take orders from women."

She gasped in momentary surprise. Then fury seized her. She stormed at him. "How dare ye defy me, ye miscreant! Ye addle-brained churl! Ye goatish knave!" With every insult hurled, her voice grew louder. "Ye mewling, odiferous, spotted toad!"

Eyes wide as saucers, the nasty little man turned tail and ran, pushing the poor beasts with the sorry job of pulling his wagon of spoiled goods as hard as he could. Alex liked to believe it was her fierce stance and sharp tongue that had chased him away, although she knew the accompanying effect of Gavin and Finlay unsheathing their broad swords may have contributed to the peddler's flight.

A piercing cry brought Alex's thoughts back to the present.

She smiled. "Wee Hamish's wails are as strong as ever," she said, leaning to see past Helen to the baby now awake in his cradle. "It would appear as though duty calls to us both," Alex said before pressing a kiss to Helen's cheek. "I'm off. I've still many families left to visit." She looked down at Will who sat on the floor surrounded by Helen's wee ones. He was handing out the rag babies Alex had found in a village shop on her return journey.

"Come along, Will," she said, standing. Then she turned back to Helen. "We've brought bread and cheese for the men in the fields. 'Tis nigh time for the noon meal."

Helen stood and scooped Hamish into her arms. "Apparently so," she said with a wink. "Now, make sure that husband of mine stops to eat. I swear he's more apt to fly to the top of Torna Doon than to squeeze in time for a meal when there's work to be done."

Alex nodded in agreement. "Gregor is hard working to be sure, but ye're right. He'll do himself ill if he doesn't rest. Ye've my word. He will sit, even if only for a quick bite."

When Alex and Will resumed their progress down the village path, she decided to have Will carry on with the rounds on his own while she brought the men in the fields the bread and cheese.

"Welcome home, Alex," Gregor called out, in between issuing curt commands to the oxen as he steered their course. Alex set the food down beside the field that had been left fallow all spring and summer and now was being turned before winter. She darted toward the men, her feet sinking into the cool earth.

"'Tis time to stop for dinner," Alex said.

Owen, one of Corc's many grandsons, smiled. "Whoa," he said, pulling on the oxen's reins.

"What do ye think ye're doing?" Gregor snapped at the younger man. "Do ye think the soil is going to turn itself?"

Alex muscled up to Gregor and thrust a finger in his face. "He's listening to his lady, is what he's doing." She held her fierce pose as long as she could before she burst out laughing. Gregor joined in, his mop of red curls bouncing while he laughed. "Let me guess," he said, catching his breath. "Ye paid a visit to Helen before stopping by."

Alex shrugged. "I might have. Anyway," she said, grabbing Owen by the upper arm and thrusting him at Gregor. "Look at this lad, he's nigh starving to death." The laughter renewed at her jest, for Owen stood a head taller than Gregor and was as broad as a bull despite only having eighteen years to his credit.

"I yield," Gregor said. "I wouldn't want to be the cause of Owen not gaining another stone by the end of the day."

Smiling, she helped them disable the plough and remove the yoke from the team so that the beasts could graze for a spell while they enjoyed their own meal.

"And how were the monks this time?" Gregor asked, handing her a large piece of bread. Her stomach rumbled, and so she happily accepted. There was plenty to go around. Soon, the men tending the crops in surrounding fields joined them.

"They were all well. Did anything happen here while I was away?" she asked.

"Some of Malcolm's sheep were pinched," Owen said before taking a bite of cheese.

Alex sat up straighter. "No one told me. Who's responsible?"

Gregor shrugged. "Tinkers most likely."

"My lady," a deep voice said behind her, the owner of which she did not doubt was Michael. He was the only MacKenzie who called her 'my lady'.

She groaned softly.

"Ye're in trouble now," Gregor said in a quiet singsong voice.

"Gregor MacKenzie, ye must have seen him coming," she hissed softly. "Ye could've warned me."

"Nay," he said, chuckling. "This was more fun."

She looked down at her dirt smeared tunic and filthy toes and whispered, "What? Do ye think Michael will find something objectionable?"

"Good morrow," the steward of Luthmore castle said, drawing near.

Shielding her eyes from the noon sun, Alex squinted up at him. "Can I assume ye're not here to join our picnic?"

Michael rolled his eyes. "Stand up, my lady, and dust yerself off. There's a dispute to settle."

Alex sighed and reached for a hunk of cheese. She took a bite and with her mouth full said to the men, "Duty calls."

"A cow eats with more manners," Michael scolded.

Alex stood up and patted him on the back. "Do not fash yerself. Ye know I clean up fine and can be as enchanting as I please, when I please." A hiccup intruded upon her speech.

"Aye, ye're a vision," Michael said dryly. "Come on. Even though ye may not look or sound like Lady MacKenzie, Lady MacKenzie is needed just the same."

# Chapter Four

A lex walked into the kitchens and collapsed in a chair in the corner.

"Don't get too comfy there, Alex. My own legs are about to give way."

Alex smiled at Jean, Luthmore's cook, who bustled about the room, wiping counters and issuing orders to servants hastening to and fro, her legs looking nothing like limbs about to give way. Closing her eyes, Alex released a slow breath and rested her head against the cold stone wall behind her.

"Aw, pet."

Surprised by the sudden closeness of Jean's voice, Alex opened her eyes and looked up into the cook's soft brown eyes framed by her plump cherub face.

She gently cupped Alex's cheek with her dimpled hand. "I can tell ye've had a long day. Why don't ye take yerself to bed?"

Alex smiled and rolled forward, resting her head in her hands. Then she sat up straight and inhaled deeply. Blowing out her breath, willing her fatigue to follow the same course, she lunged to her feet. "There's no peace for the wicked," she said, stretching her arms above her head.

Jean chuckled. "Ye're about as wicked as a newborn puppy."

Alex smiled and pressed a kiss to her cheek. "Ye only believe that because ye don't know about my secret life, smuggling coin and riding alongside outlaws."

Jean's laughter rang out. "Och, but ye're incorrigible. Can ye imagine what stuffy ol' Michael would say if he heard the jests ye make. He's angry enough with ye going around barefoot like ye do. Secret life," she said, shaking her head and hooting with laughter. "Smuggling coin, riding alongside outlaws. Aye, that would set him on his ear right enough."

Jean wiped her eyes and took hold of Alex's hand. "No one has ever made me laugh harder than ye, pet." An instant later her smile vanished. "Mind ye don't tell Michael that I don't chastise ye more. I'd never hear the end of his complaints. Always telling me to not encourage yer common ways, he is. 'She's the lady of Clan MacKenzie'" Jean said, imitating Michael's disapproving tones.

Alex clasped her hands together, feigning a look of contrition. "We've likely risked Michael's anger enough with all this impious laughter." She stood up and hooked arms with Jean. "Let us play the role of dutiful lady and cook. We must inspect the stores and plan the menu for Lammas before I go to the chapel for my evening prayers. I've tarried too long as it is."

Jean pressed her hand to her bosom. "Why are ye so anxious to pray? Is something amiss?"

Alex pressed her lips together to suppress a smile. Jean tended to panic at the slightest hint of trouble.

"Calm yerself," Alex said while gently leading the older woman toward the kitchen stores. "Naught is amiss. I simply do not wish to retire too late to visit my father. I have not seen him since my return."

After carefully inspecting the inventory, they decided on venison stew to finish off the meat from the most recent hunt and fried herring with creamed chestnuts. Then she made a pass through the buttery. When she was satisfied with the barrel count, Alex left the kitchens through the servant's entrance and made her way to the castle chapel. Situated separately from the keep, yet still enclosed within the courtyard, the small kirk was Alex's haven. Upon entering, the coolness and quiet of the chapel soothed her soul, and she felt the harried pace of the day slip away as peace enveloped her.

It was her mother who had instilled in her the need to pray in the evenings before bed. Alana had stressed the importance, not only to show gratitude for the clan's blessings and to pray for their continued wellbeing, but also for the benefit and health of Alex herself. She closed her eyes, and for a moment she was a child again, her small hand safely nestled inside her mother's while they knelt together in front of the altar.

*"Mama, 'tis so dark." Alex's gaze flitted over the walls, which were alive with dancing shadows from the flickering candlelight. She thought of the ghost stories her friend, Helen, had told her and Mary in the village earlier that day.*

*Her mother's violet gaze locked with hers. "Candlelight is peaceful, Alex, and peace is why we are here. Listen closely to what I say, for yer life will be forever one of service to yer people. As lady of the keep, the welfare of the clan is yer responsibility, a responsibility that will be more taxing with each passing year. Someday, ye may resent the sacrifice, which will lead ye down a selfish road—one where ye may come to believe the people are here to serve ye. To protect yer people from yerself, ye must come to the chapel every night and give yer worries up to God."*

*Then Alana handed Alex a chain, from which hung a silver trinity knot. "Wear this always. It was my mother's and now I give it to ye. It symbolizes the Father, the Son, and the Holy Spirit but also the Maid, the Mother, and the Crone, and ye, Alex—yer mind, yer body, and yer spirit. Keep yer faith in God. Hold close*

*the council of women, and never lose faith in yerself. Remember*
*my words, and ye'll honor this one truth—the wellbeing of the*
*people comes first, always."*

Alex pressed her eyes shut and smiled, hearing her mother's
voice in her mind and remembering the feel of her touch. With
Alana close in her heart, she knelt in the dimly lit kirk and
closed her eyes. With each breath she inhaled, she invited acceptance into her heart to calm her restless soul, and with every
exhale, she expelled fear and doubt.

Feeling refreshed, she left her haven and made her way to
her father's solar. The one candle she carried provided the only
light when she entered the spacious circular room. "Da, 'tis so
dark in here."

"I like the dark," a low, quiet voice said in answer.

"Nonsense," Alex scolded as she crossed the large room to
her father's bedside and lit the candles on his nightstand.

"It suits me in my crippled state," he said.

"All the more reason to keep yer curtains open in the day
and candles lit at night. It will improve yer spirits, Da. Trust
me."

With the room properly illuminated, Alex turned and sat
down beside her father, taking his hand in hers.

"Ah, sweetling," he said, but then his brow suddenly furrowed. "Why is it that I feel I've not seen ye for an age?"

She pressed a kiss to the back of his hand. "I've not been
gone an age, but ye're right, I have been away this last month."

"Oh," he said. "And where did ye go?"

Alex pressed her lips together to push down the ache that
threatened to grip her heart. No matter how much time passed,
she would never grow accustomed to her father's limitations.

On the eve before she left, she had told him about her journey to Haddington. On the day she left, she had said goodbye. She knew every night in her absence, Mary would have sat with her father in her stead and told him that Alex had gone to visit the abbot, and still he had no recollection of her journey. Breathing deeply, she rejected the anxiety that threatened to build within her. She would hold fast to her peace and give her worry for her father up to God.

Smiling, she said, "I've just returned from visiting Abbot Matthew."

A slow smile lit his drawn features. "How is the abbot?"

"He is well. It was a quiet, uneventful visit." She fought the need to make the sign of the cross. Lying to her father made her feel wretched, but regretfully it could not be helped. If he knew that she had smuggled a small fortune sewn into her dress over several leagues...alone...meeting with strange men in the woods...alone, he would never allow her to leave her chambers again. He might even suddenly regain the strength to walk just so that he could march her to her rooms and lock her away. Of course, come tomorrow, he would completely forget her confession.

"Ye're such a good lass."

She groaned inwardly as she recalled how she had asked a Scottish rebel to undress her while another man looked on. Then she sat straighter, pushing aside her guilt. After all, how else was she going to remove her surcote? Reckless acts were committed every day in the name of Scottish independence. And although she was a woman, like so many brave Scotsmen, she had heard the call. More than that, because of her aid, Abbot Matthew had the coin to start rebuilding the Scottish cavalry. She may have behaved scandalously, but it was all for King and country. Then a flash of sky-blue eyes and full lips passed before her mind's eye, and she remembered boldly grabbing Rory's tunic and pressing her lips hard and wantonly against his. All right—so she had to concede that some of her scandalous behavior was not for Scotland, but how was she to resist those lips?

"I'm sorry, Father," she blurted.

"What for?" he said, looking bemused.

She hesitated and then simply smiled, brushing his hair away from his brow. "For always fussing so much."

"I don't remember complaining. I like when ye fuss over me. Yer mother used to fuss whenever I got the slightest bit ill. I admit it always pleased me. Anyway, ye digress. What of the abbot?"

Alex smiled. "He is well and vows to journey here to Luthmore before the year's end."

Rare laughter escaped her father's lips, the sound quiet but unmistakably full of mirth. "What mischief Matthew and I got up to as lads." He looked at Alex. "Would ye believe it if I told ye he'd bested me with the sword time and again?"

Her eyes widened with surprise. "Ye never told me that. I can hardly imagine the good abbot wielding a sword."

She leaned down and pressed a kiss to his forehead. The cool temperature pleased her. So often fevers laid claim to his weakened body, each time stealing away a little more of his dwindling vitality. He reached up with his frail hand and grazed her cheek.

"I love ye, Da," she whispered, kissing his cheek. Then she sat back, but her mother's necklace had laced around his fingers and snapped when she pulled away.

"Oh dear," he said, realizing what had occurred.

Her heart ached at the sight of the broken chain, but she masked her feelings to protect her father.

"Do not fash yerself, Da. 'Twas an accident. I can fix it." She eased back in her chair, rubbing the trinity knot between her fingers. Then she motioned to the untouched piece of bread and full bowl of broth on the other nightstand. "Did ye eat at all today?"

"Aye, feasts and feasts. Jean can hardly keep up with me."

"Liar," she shot back. Taking the bread, and dipping it in the broth, she held it up to his lips. "Come on, Da, one bite?"

He shook his head, grimacing. "Nay, lass. My stomach pains me." He closed his eyes, his voice strained. "And I'm tired, so tired."

"Then sleep, Da," she said, standing. "We'll break our fast together in the morning."

But he reached out and grabbed her hand. "Nay, lass. My own, sweet lass. Stay with me a while."

"Nay, Da. Ye must rest."

"Alex," he said, the barest hint of a smile curving his lips. "Just sit with me and keep talking."

She slowly sat back down. "What would be like to talk about?"

He held her hand in his cold one. "I just want to hear yer voice. Tell me anything. Just...just keep talking."

"All right, Da. I'll stay a while." She climbed into bed beside him and rested her head on his shoulder like she had when she was child and told her da about the new slippers she had bought at market for Mary and how beautiful the countryside looked on her return journey north, and how the heather had at last bloomed. It was not long until he had drifted off to sleep. She held him a while, remembering earlier days when his body had been strong and his mind sharp. She remembered the security she had once felt when both her parents had been alive.

Pressing a kiss to his forehead, she rose from the bed and moved to stand beside the casement. She pulled back the tapestry and looked out over the moors, painted violet by twilight's brush. She saw the outline of cottages and the expanse of the MacKenzie village, and the cliffs of Torna Doon in the distance. Then she strained to see what was beyond, to the numerous families who lived scattered along the vast MacKenzie territory. So many people relied on her. As her mother forewarned, the weight of responsibility settled on her shoulders. If she allowed it to weigh her down, she would taste resentment. But she thrust her shoulders back and bravely raised her chin. She would carry on as the true acting chieftain of the MacKenzie, even if none of the world knew.

IN THE MORNING, SHE awoke and remembered her promise to her father to break their fast together. Alex hurried to the kitchen and helped Jean assemble a tray with fresh baked bread, a bowl of hot broth and a vase of his favorite flowers, mountain Avens, whose white petals curved like small bowls with yellow centers.

She balanced the tray with one hand and opened the door to her father's solar with the other. The tapestries hanging over the windows blotted out the cheer of summer's morning. She set the tray down on his nightstand and crossed to the windows. "Since ye cannot walk outside, let me bring the outside to ye," she said, sweeping the tapestries aside.

Smiling, she returned to his bedside and reached for one of the white flowers, bringing the petals to his nose. "These were picked just this morning."

Donnan remained asleep.

She returned the flower to its vase and started to butter a piece of the bread for him. "Wake up, Da. Ye won't believe the gossip I overheard from the servants in the kitchen." She paused to reach for a small bowl. "Do ye want some stewed baeberries on yer bread?"

She waited, but her father didn't answer. "Come on, Da. 'Tis time to wake."

Still, he did not answer.

"Da?" She leaned closer and saw that his lips were curved in the slightest smile.

"Very funny, Da." She cupped his cheek and gasped. His skin was cold to her touch. Her eyes widened. She lunged forward, pulling away the bedclothes. "Da," she shouted, shaking him, trying to wake him.

"Da!"

Then the truth slowly seeped into her unwilling mind.

Donnan, Laird of the MacKenzie, was dead.

She climbed into bed beside him just as she had done the night before and wept with her head resting on his shoulder.

# Chapter Five

Alex planted her feet firmly on the cold, stone floor of the great hall, despite the throbbing ache drumming at her toes and heels. Refusing to yield to her fatigue and the weight of her grief, she stood, receiving her kinsmen one by one.

Corc, stooped with age, slowly climbed the steps to the high dais and eased stiffly down on one knee in front her. With his head bowed, she strained to hear the words that rasped from his tremulous lips.

"My lady, with gratitude I served yer father, yer father's father, and I can even recall the days of yer great grandfather's chiefdom. Happy and blessed are we who have basked beneath the kind justice of their light."

Alex squatted down and gently clasped the old man's hands. Imbuing her gaze with a warmth her grieving heart could not feel, she smiled and whispered their clan motto. "*Luceo non uro.*" I shine not burn.

Corc looked up then and met her gaze. His red-rimmed, faded-blue eyes brimmed with tears. "No light has ever shined brighter than ye, Alex," he said, his chin quivering.

Alex gently squeezed his hands. "Ye're too good to me by far, Corc. May all the angels and all the saints bless yer sweet heart." Helping him stand, she pressed a kiss to his wrinkled cheek before handing him off to Michael, who helped him shuffle back down the stairs.

She turned once more to face the line of kinfolk just as a mop of red hair raced at her. Before she could draw her next breath, Cassie's slim, wee arms encircled her waist in a cling-ing embrace. Alex's heart broke a little more when she looked down into the child's big, tearful eyes.

"Oh, sweetling! Don't cry, dear lass," Alex crooned, swiping Cassie's cheeks, her own heartache momentarily forgotten in the presence of Cassie's innocent pain.

Helen came forward then, her nose red, tears freely stream-ing down her cheeks. "I tried to keep her at home. But when she found out that yer da died, the poor dear has not stopped sobbing."

Swallowing the fresh knot of tears pushing up her throat, Alex looked back down at Cassie. "Ye and me both," she whis-pered.

"I'm so sorry, Alex," Helen said. Then she shifted her gaze to Mary who stood at Alex's side. "I hope he did not suffer."

"We do not think he did," Mary said, her voice thick with tears.

Alex drew a deep breath, fighting to remain composed. "He passed in his sleep." Her voice broke, releasing a well of tears be-yond the barriers of her control.

Helen pulled both Alex and Mary into a crushing embrace.

"There, there," Helen crooned softly. "Ye both cry all ye want. There's no finer man than Donnan; a sea of tears would not be too many to spend on the likes of him."

"Helen," Michael said, also drawing Alex's gaze. "Perhaps ye can convince Alexandria to rest for a spell."

Mary wiped her tears and nodded. "Please, Alex. If not rest, then at least some food and drink." Then Mary turned to He-len. "She hasn't eaten all day, nor has she sat, not once."

Helen cupped Alex's cheeks. "The line of mourners yet extends beyond the courtyard gates. Ye're no good to anyone if ye faint from hunger."

"Where's William?" Alex asked Michael.

"He's gone riding with Gavin to race off some of his grief."

Alex's gaze shifted to Mary. Her cousin's face was a composition of worry and pain. Slowly, Alex nodded. "I will not sit, but I will have some broth."

Michael disappeared and reappeared in a flash with a bowl in hand, along with a hearty crust of bread. He motioned to her father's imposing high-backed chair. "Sit just while ye eat, my lady."

She shook her head, planting her feet wider with new resolve. "That chair will stay empty until it is rightfully filled."

Michael bowed his head. "And so it shall, my lady."

Alex moved away from the others with her food. For hours, she had stood receiving her kin—not just the villagers living within the protection of Luthmore but also the cottars scattered across the countryside. Days would pass before the entire clan had come to bid farewell to their beloved laird.

She glanced at the empty chair, and then out across the sea of villagers. Whether conjured by her despair or images of truth, she thought she noticed some of the men eying her father's seat overly long while whispering to those who stood nearby. She imagined what they said...

*There is no heir—only she. Who will fill that chair?* Did each man want it for himself?

Whipping wind barreled through the open doors into the great hall, lifting her hair off her shoulders. She whirled around, her eyes drawn to the wind's source. The banner of the

MacLeod appeared, followed by a man of great height with broad shoulders and cold, hard eyes. Behind him followed another man of equal stature, scanning the room with the same harsh gaze. A heavy pulse of thick dread coursed through her. She had known her neighbors would call, but she had not believed they would call so soon. She turned and motioned for a servant, quickly handing off the sustenance she had barely tasted. Then she returned to stand in the middle of the high dais right in front of her father's chair.

Gordon MacLeod strode past the line of villagers. Her pulse raced harder. She was weary. The weight of grief bogged down her mind, sapping her strength. She was not ready for a standoff with the MacLeod, but that did not matter—it couldn't matter. Her people needed her to be strong, and that is what she would do. Steeling her courage, she widened her stance and looked the MacLeod boldly in the eye as he stopped at the foot of the stairs. Despite being on higher ground, his great height reduced the impact of her strategic placement. Still, she elongated her back to claim every advantage of her position. She wanted to rid her people of fear. She wanted them to feel secure in the absence of their laird, especially in that moment of intense, vulnerable grief. Fear was all too easy a pathway to turn down when hearts were broken.

"Gordon MacLeod," she said, speaking first. "Ye have come, I ken, to pay yer respects to my father and my kin."

The MacLeod dipped his head to her, his brow pinched with a sadness that did not reach his eyes. "Clan MacLeod mourns the passing of Donnan MacKenzie," he said loudly for all to hear.

She clenched her fists. He clearly wished to convey his own message to her people.

The MacLeod turned then, showing her his back, and raised his hand to beckon the attention of everyone in the great hall. "But Clan Mackenzie, know this—while yer chieftain's chair is empty—I vow to safeguard yer borders." Then he turned and looked pointedly at Alex, placing his hand on his son's shoulder and said, his voice still projecting across the great hall. "My son, Eudard, is strong. He's a warrior. He will watch over ye."

Alex tensed as she locked eyes with Eudard MacLeod. An arrogant smile curved his lips. She stiffened. The Laird of the MacLeod had just implied a match between herself and Eudard. The idea of binding her people to a leader as hard and ruthless as Gordon MacLeod made her stomach twist. She had to fight to suppress the disgust from appearing on her face. Drawing a deep breath, she spoke loudly to ensure her voice carried to every villager. "Clan MacLeod is strong, but so too is Clan MacKenzie. I've heard tell, Gordon MacLeod, that ye've already committed the strength of yer clan elsewhere by forming an alliance with Lord Ruddington, who sits not seven leagues from here in a castle that does not belong to him." As she spoke, her confidence grew. She stepped down one step, bring herself eye to eye with the MacLeod. "I presume then that yer son will be occupied safeguarding the Englishman's borders."

The MacLeod's nostrils flared at her refusal of his implied proposal. "Lord Ruddington sends his condolences, and if Clan MacKenzie were to give their allegiance to King Edward,

Lord Ruddington and his many knights would provide yer clan with protection and greater wealth."

She wanted to rail at him. How could he betray Scotland? But she knew she was not in a position to provoke the ire of the MacLeod. "We have long protected our own borders and will continue to do so. Our allegiance is to Scotland. I thank ye for yer sympathies." She turned to Michael. "See that Laird MacLeod and his son enjoy MacKenzie hospitality and provide them with supplies to ensure a fine journey home." Then she curtsied before turning on her heel and striding away with her head held high. The moment she passed behind the screen, which concealed the stairs to the family rooms, her knees felt like they would give way. Her heart thundered in her ears. She had held her own, but it had cost everything. She scurried up the stairs so that she might break down in private.

MICHAEL STOOD JUST outside the solar and listened to Alex's sobs. He wanted to comfort her, but having known the lass her whole life, he knew had he shown himself, she would have choked back her tears and swallowed her pain. He shook his head, regretting the enormity of pressure weighted on her young shoulders. For years now, she had been the acting laird of Clan MacKenzie, but always in secret. Now that her father was dead, she would feel the full weight of that responsibility. The eyes of the clan were on her, watching, hoping, waiting—but there was only so much a woman could do. And the presence of the MacLeod today made it clear that everyone was very aware that Clan MacKenzie had no man to assume the role of chieftain. This had to be remedied, and sooner rather than later, but now was not the time. He also knew it was essential that Alex be allowed to grieve.

Michael's opportunity to discuss Alex's need for a husband came just two days after the Laird's funeral. He sought her in her solar to discuss the harvest. Once everything had been addressed, Michael cleared his throat. "My lady, we need to discuss what happened when Laird MacLeod came to...uh...pay his respects."

Alex stood in a huff and crossed to the mantle, taking down her father's sword. "Pay his respects? That's a very polite way of saying circling for the kill."

"Aye, well that, too. The point is, ye were right." Michael cleared his throat again as he crossed the room. "Clan MacKenzie has always protected its borders. We do not need the MacLeod or King Edward's protection." He paused, waiting for her to look at him. When her eyes locked with his, he said, "But the clan does need a chieftain."

Her nostrils flared. "I have been this clan's chieftain for the past three years."

Michael nodded. "Aye, ye have, but in secret. Alexandria, ye're still a woman."

With a fierce yelp, she swung the heavy sword and brought it down on the mantle, its blade sinking into the wood. Breathless, she yanked the sword free and turned to face him. "I ken ye're right." She leaned the sword against the wall and expelled a long breath. "There's no way around it. I'll just have to find myself a husband."

She crossed to a side table and poured two cups of wine. Handing one to Michael, she gestured toward the high-backed chairs facing the cold hearth and said, "My father is dead. 'Tis up to us to sort the matter now."

She sat down and sipped the wine. "So," she said.

Next to her, Michael cleared his throat. "So," he said in reply.

"A husband," she muttered before taking another sip.

"Aye, a husband," he repeated.

Frustrated, she set her cup down and scooted to the edge of her seat, turning to face Michael. "This shouldn't be so difficult. 'Tis only a husband. Ladies secure husbands every day."

Michael shifted in his seat, mirroring her body language. "Right," he said. "'Tis just a husband."

She stood up then and started pacing in front of the hearth. "Exactly. We just need a man. Any man should do. Why not any one of the MacKenzie warriors."

Michael shook his head. "Nay, my lady. The MacLeod offered ye his son, and ye publicly rejected him. If ye were to now marry a commoner, doubtless ye'd start a feud. We are the stronger clan, but ye don't want to go looking for trouble."

She stopped dead in front of Michael, her hands on her hips. "I'm not marrying Eudard MacLeod. He is a beast of a man."

"I agree, my lady. But having just received his offer, albeit indirectly, ye now must marry someone of noble birth." Michael raked his hand through his hair. "After Robin died, yer father should have betrothed ye to another man straightaway. Now what do we do? I haven't the slightest idea how to go about finding ye a husband."

Alex sat down again. "I can do it."

"Ye," Michael snorted. "What are ye going to do? Solicit lords and clan chieftains on yer own behalf."

She slumped back in her chair. "I suppose ye're right." Then a moment later she jumped to her feet. "I've got it. Abbot Matthew!"

Michael frowned. "Ye can't marry the abbot."

Alex laughed out loud for the first time in days. "Michael, I think ye're the one who needs rest. What I meant is that Abbot Matthew can find me a husband." She crossed to the large table on the other side of the room. "I will write to him straightaway and tell him all that has occurred."

She took up her quill and began to compose her letter, pausing only when she heard Michael sigh dramatically. She looked up, meeting his gaze.

He shook his head before downing his portion of wine. "Matchmaking monks—this is bound to go well."

# Chapter Six

"Whoa," Rory said, bringing his horse to a halt in front of the Ankeld village blacksmith. He was greeted by the thick, shifting back muscles of Ramsay McDonough who stood, legs spread, pumping the bellows. Ramsay's fire roared and burned brighter with every life-giving breath. Then with tongs, he retrieved a long, slim piece of tortured metal from the flames, red hot and ready to submit to the command of Ramsay's hammer. He turned then, strands of blond hair clinging to his forehead, and brought metal to anvil, while at the same time reaching for his hammer. Down it came. The sharp clang rang out, piercing the air.

"*Alba gu bràth*, Ramsay," Rory said when next the hammer head reached toward the sky.

Ramsay looked up, a scowl of surprise darkening his pale blue eyes the instant before a crooked smile bade Rory welcome. His hammer slammed down again. The hot metal yielded, shedding sparks like tears. Tongs pinched tightly, Ramsay removed the flattened piece and drove it into a bucket of water. Steam billowed off the surface as heat and flame surrendered to their master.

Setting his hammer down, Ramsay reached out his hand, which Rory firmly clasped in greeting. "Go ahead," the blacksmith said, gesturing deeper inside his stall toward a narrow door. "He's waiting on ye."

Rory nodded. "As always, ye have my thanks." Before he crossed to the door, he glanced at the road. Villagers crowded the busy streets, heading toward the green where the market had been assembled.

"Ye're all right," Ramsay said, reassuringly. "Go ahead."

Rory ducked his head beneath the overhang and retreated into the shadows of the dim stall toward the door. Once inside, he walked past crates filled with tools, then behind a large stack of wood. Squatting low, he squeezed his fingers beneath one of the wooden floor planks. It came loose. Setting it aside, he did the same with the next, wider plank, creating enough space for his large frame to squeeze through. Darkness greeted him as he stepped down through the hole, his head still remaining above the floor. He had to duck to move the planks back in place, concealing himself beneath. Then, staying low, he turned to his right and took three long strides, which brought him to a short, arched passageway from the top of which hung a thick blue curtain. Pushing the fabric aside, he descended a small staircase into a narrow room, illuminated by two fat candles. At the far end sat a keg propped up on a stool with several tankards stacked on top. Above the keg hung a wooden sign, which read The Iron Shoe Tavern, and dominating the space was a narrow table with six wooden chairs.

At the far end of the table, the abbot sat, busy scribbling on a piece of parchment. He looked up and waved Rory over, then motioned to a tankard placed in front of the chair at his side. "I've poured yer cup."

Rory slumped into the chair, his legs spread wide. He wiped at his eyes before stretching his neck from side to side.

"Ye made good time," Abbot Matthew said.

A lazy smile curved Rory's lips. "I rode like I was outrunning the devil himself, pardon any blasphemy."

The abbot, his smile unwavering, cocked a brow at Rory. "Given yer outstanding work for a higher cause, I'm quite certain the good Lord will forgive ye. Although as ye know, I cannot hear confession. Ye'll need a priest for that."

Rory sat straight and reached for his cup, taking a long draught. His eyes followed the candle smoke coiling in thin ribbons through the floorboards into Ramsay's stall above their heads, combining undetected with the ubiquitous cloud and soot of the blacksmith's fire. The Iron Shoe Tavern was Ramsay's contribution to the cause. Originally extra storage, he'd turned his cellar into a safe meeting place for the abbot's agents. The clash of striking metal began again, absorbing Rory and Abbot Matthew's conversation. Rory took another sip of ale and smiled. Ramsay even ensured they did not go thirsty.

The abbot had returned his attention to his paper, deftly composing words in his even, disciplined hand.

Rory stood to refill his cup. "Ye must have been mighty pleased by the last fortune of silver David delivered."

The abbot nodded but did not look up. "Indeed. I intend to purchase chargers to rebuild the Scottish cavalry."

Rory sat back, enjoying his relaxed surroundings while the sharp ringing of the hammer kept watch. "I have to tell ye, Abbot. I enjoyed that last mission in particular."

This time the abbot looked up and seemed to consider Rory for a moment. "Judging by the less than holy twinkle in yer eye, I feel it's safe to assume ye met Alex."

Rory leaned forward, elbows on the table and raked his hands through his hair. "Met her? Abbot, I undressed her."

The abbot winced. "Och, knowing ye both as I do, I am not surprised to hear that, not surprised at all." Frowning, he sat back in his seat and scratched at his shorn head. "Ye know, 'tis interesting that ye should bring Alex up, because she's central to the reason I summoned ye here."

Rory sat forward, an alarm sounding in his mind. Being an agent for Scotland was dangerous. On any given day, every one of the abbot's agents risked capture, injury, and most certainly death. "What's happened? Is she hurt? Was she arrested?"

The abbot shook his head, putting up a pacifying hand. "Nay, nothing like that, lad. She's not in immediate danger; however, she is in trouble and has turned to me for aid."

The tension eased somewhat from Rory's shoulders. "What are the particulars?"

"Her father recently passed away; may God rest his soul."

"God rest his soul," Rory repeated, making the sign of the cross with the abbot. "I'm sorry to hear that."

"Aye, he was a good man. Unfortunately, he didn't settle the matter of her marriage before he passed away."

"Forgive me for saying so, but can marriage be so important to one of yer agents, to a rebel—even if she is a woman?"

"It is if the agent's father is laird of Clan MacKenzie."

"Laird?" Rory blurted. He sat back and blew out a long breath. Images of the Alex MacKenzie he had met came rushing back to him, her slender form, her request for him to untie her laces, her cheeky smile, her strong thigh with a dagger strapped to it. "Are ye quite certain we are talking about the same woman?"

The abbot chuckled. "Alex flouts convention to be sure. Remember, the most ruthless of nobles can often be the most polite or well-behaved. Alex has never been well-behaved. She aspires to reach far higher ideals."

"Did her father know of her involvement with the cause?"

The abbot shook his head. "No one knows that I'm aware of, although I would not be surprised if her cousin, Mary, guarded her secret."

"Is there not someone else with the authority to select her husband, a brother or an uncle?"

"There is no one, and that, my lad, is the problem. Clan MacKenzie has no chieftain. Her father's chair sits empty while those who would claim it wait for the opportune moment. Already she feels pressed by the MacLeod, a neighboring chieftain. The wealth of the clan, the desirability of their land—'tis too fine a prize for even the best intentioned to resist. There will be others who will want the wealth for themselves. Worse yet, Gordon MacLeod is in league with the English. Tensions in the region are bound to rise, placing Alex at their perilous center."

"What's to be done?"

"Before committing my life to the service of God, I was a MacKenzie. It is my duty to ensure the clan remains safe while a husband is chosen for her. To that end, I am sending three men north to MacKenzie territory. Each man is good and loyal to Scotland, not to mention highly skilled at specific elements of defense. They will ensure the MacKenzie warriors have the support and training needed to handle any possible attacks."

"What about me? Why am I here?" Rory asked.

"Ye're here for Scotland," the abbot said, leaning closer. "Alex has a stockpile of weapons hidden away. I am sending ye north so that ye can help her bring those weapons to me."

"Weapons, ye say? I was just speaking to David about that very subject." Rory smiled as he considered the prospect of another mission with Alex MacKenzie. Wetting his lips, he leaned forward. "When do I leave?"

# Chapter Seven

Rory lagged a little behind the three other men as they rode across the long, narrow bridge toward the outer battlements of Luthmore castle. He had chosen to remain on the periphery of their group for the duration of the journey north. It was not that Rory disliked the others. After all, Abbot Matthew's estimation of character was never made lightly. If he had chosen Adam, Robert, and Timothy to provide the MacKenzie warriors with support in the absence of a laird, then Rory had to trust they were each worthy of the task. And over the last two days, he had judged them all to be decent sort of men and loyal to Scotland. Still, they were noblemen.

As the son of peasants, Rory had spent little time in the company of gentry. In fact, the only time he had ever spoken to noblemen or women was when he and his brothers had been robbing them. Rory smiled, remembering those not-too-distant days. Their gang had been called the Saints—the name chosen by an authority higher even than the abbot—so named by the bishop himself. In fact, it was the bishop who had given them the swords and black masks that had sent terror into the hearts of those English nobles who were unlucky enough to meet the Saints on the rode north into Scotland. Not that their terror was reasonably grounded. The Saints had adhered to a simple code; they were thieves not murderers. More than that, they were not even truly thieves. Their stolen gains were never kept for themselves—every coin, jewel, or trinket fed the cause.

It was Scotland's money. The Saints were only taking back what was rightfully theirs.

Of course, the men in his company now were unlike the English nobles who had stared down the length of the Saints' blades. They were Scotsmen, allies, and brothers-at-arms. Still, he did not feel entirely at ease with them. Timothy and Robert, both good men, seemed rather odd to him, and Adam, although overall of decent character, possessed an underlying arrogance, as if he was used to giving orders and having men obey.

At least they were almost to Luthmore Castle. Rory bit the inside of his cheek to silence the laughter bubbling in his throat at the sight of Timothy once more dropping his reins and making the sign of the cross. Rory was certainly not an ungodly man, but it was at least the tenth time Timothy had released his reins to pray just that morning. Rory had never questioned the abbot's wisdom, and he was not about to start, but he could not imagine what Timothy would teach Alex's Highland warriors.

As if conjured by Rory's question, a large, fierce looking man with an enormous broad sword strapped to his back and clad in naught but a plaid rode out to meet them.

"Who are ye? And what business have ye at Luthmore?" the Highlander growled.

Rory kept his distance. It was the other men who had business with the whole MacKenzie clan, and one of them was in possession of a letter to prove it. Rory was there to see only one MacKenzie, the lady of the keep, and he too had a special letter in his satchel. But it was for Alex's eyes only. A pleasurable warmth flooded his chest at the prospect of seeing her again. He sat back in his saddle and watched Adam nudge his horse forward and dismount in front of the guard.

"We've been sent by Abbot Matthew of Haddington Abbey to bring his condolences to the lady Alexandria and to Clan MacKenzie. We are to be of service to her in this her hour of need." Adam withdrew a small square of parchment from his saddlebag. Rory was not surprised to see that it was Adam who carried the missive from the abbot. "I have a letter for the captain of the MacKenzie guard with the abbot's seal to prove the truth of my claim. Are ye Gavin MacKenzie?"

The large Highlander relaxed his stance. "I am," he said, stretching out his hand for the letter. After examining it, he held it up for everyone to see. Oddly, there were no written words, but then Rory realized the abbot must have guessed that Gavin MacKenzie would not be able to read. Instead, a likeness of the MacKenzie coat of arms filled the page, and at its center was the seal of the abbot.

Gavin smiled. "Ye're all most welcome. I pray ye provide our lady with whatever comfort ye may. She is beloved by her people and none can observe her grief without feeling the acuteness of pain in our own hearts. Her father, too, was a great man...God rest his soul."

Adam followed first behind the warrior. As the son of a lord or some other such title, it was his place. Behind Adam rode Robert—who Rory had liked well enough. He seemed to be an expert on horses, having spoken of little else on their two-day journey. After Timothy, Rory fell in line, which was fitting as he was the son of a peasant, not to mention an outlaw. More than that, Rory's position in the rear of the line suited him just fine. As an expert swordsman, the abbot sent Rory under the guise of training the MacKenzie warriors, but since that wasn't his true purpose, he wished to bring as little attention to himself as possible.

Passing through the massive MacKenzie gates, Gavin waved over a tall man, slim of build with long, white hair. Adam, Robert, and Timothy crossed the courtyard to meet him while Rory stayed back to observe. The white-haired man conversed with the visiting noblemen for several minutes before he dipped his head in a polite bow and made his way to Rory.

The man possessed shrewd blue eyes and an intelligent air. "I bid ye welcome," he began. "My name is Michael MacKenzie. I am steward of Luthmore Castle. May I know yer name, sir."

Rory smiled. "I'm not a knight or a lord. I'm as common as the ground we stand upon. I hail from Berwick where I once labored on the docks like my da before me. Ye need not call me sir."

Michael smiled in return. "Ye're a friend of the abbot's, which makes ye welcome here—title or no title." Then he motioned to the other men. "I was just telling yer traveling companions that the lady is not in the keep just now, but I expect her return forthwith—" A commotion near the gate cut Michael short.

Rory looked back in time to see a flurry of chickens and children burst into the courtyard, followed by a bigger boy with a messy mop of bright red hair and a dusty, flaxen-haired woman screeching with her hands twisted into claws of attack. "I'm going to get ye," she cried, her laughter undermining the threat.

Michael groaned, shaking his head. Rory could not help but laugh out loud. Alex was as vibrant as he remembered her, and now even more pleasing in her disheveled state: hair tangled; her threadbare tunic covered in small dirty handprints, clearly from all the hugs she received from the wee ones; her feet bare and nearly black from dirt. Michael may not have approved of Alex's appearance or demeanor, but Rory could not take his eyes off her. She was magnificent, her cheeks flushed from her exertions, her face lit with unabashed joy. She was genuine—and he was captivated.

"Lady Alexandria," Michael said loudly.

"Uh-oh, Alex. We're in trouble now," the red-haired boy said, laughing.

Alex stopped in her tracks as she sought Michael's gaze through the dust and chaos. "I ken what ye're going to say, Michael. I'm a disgrace, but I also think ye ken my reply—I don't care about the state of my tunic or my hair."

"Got ye," a wee voice called out the instant before Alex fell back onto the ground. A moment later, she was drowning beneath a sea of small arms and legs. "Ye wee beasties," she called out. "Attacking when I was distracted." She got to work tickling bellies and bare feet. Peals of tortured laughter rang out. "Save yerselves," one of the children yelled, and soon the mass dispersed.

She closed her eyes as she tried to catch her breath.

"My lady, may I help ye to yer feet?"

Alex opened her eyes. She squinted against the bright sunshine that shadowed the man above her. Then he squatted down beside her, his face instantly becoming clear. She drew in a sharp breath, but his sky-blue eyes held a warning. And the slightest shake of his head told her all she needed to know—that night in the woods had never happened. To the world around them, they were meeting for the very first time. Still, she would know that face anywhere. Her heart raced as she placed her hand in his.

"'Tis nice to meet yer acquaintance," Rory said, his voice deep and unhurried.

"The pleasure is mine," Alex said, boldly returning his gaze.

He bent lower and wrapped his arm around her waist, then lifted her to her feet. His hand did not linger, but she could still feel the imprint of warmth where he had touched her.

William moved to stand in front of Alex. She smiled down at her young protector. "This is my wee brother, William. But everyone calls him, Will."

"'Tis good to meet ye, Will," Rory said.

Michael cleared his throat, intruding upon their conversation. "My lady, ye've more guests to meet," he said, gesturing to three young men, all impeccably dressed, and each offering her a smile in greeting.

"If ye please," Rory said, once more winning her attention. "I have a letter from the abbot. He instructed me to present it to ye even before introductions were made."

Curious, Alex took the offered letter and without hesitation, she broke the abbot's seal and began to read:

*My Dearest Alexandria,*

*My heart is heavy as I too grieve for your father. As you know, Donnan was my dearest friend from youth. Never has there lived a kinder or more generous man. Take comfort knowing that he now sits with our Lord at His table. Also, please know that you are not alone. I received your letter and am fully prepared to guide you in finding a husband. Marriage is a sound choice at this time. To this end, I have sent you a selection of men, three in num-*

*ber. Each meets certain criteria that I decided would set you on a path toward marital satisfaction, although I do hope love will grow between you and whomever you select. First, none of the men are first sons. This has naturally reduced the expectation they and their families have placed on their marriages. Second, they each possess even temperaments. Third, their families have substantial wealth, and so none are driven by greed.*

*Let me provide ye with some particulars on each man:*

*Sir Adam Lennox is the third son of Lord Lennox and a knight under the Lord of Fife. Despite the shifting loyalties of his father and patron, Sir Adam's loyalty has always been to Scotland. His age is eight and twenty. He has proved himself on the battlefield and understands strategy. In the wake of several holdings in the Highlands falling into the hands of English lords, he can provide your warriors insight into the differing combat styles. Likewise, I have encouraged him to study your Highland warriors to strengthen the skills of our lowlander soldiers.*

*Robert is also eight and twenty and is the wealthy son of a horse breeder in Edinburgh. He was knighted two years ago by the Lord of Menteith. Like his father, he is also an expert on horses. His interest and knowledge borders on obsession, but if you heed his advice, the MacKenzie horses will be the finest in the Highlands. Robert is there to assist your stable master and to train your warriors for the cavalry. This, as you know, also supports the cause, as we are rebuilding our army during this truce. He will bring one of his prize horses and will trade the stud for one of the MacKenzie's.*

*Timothy is four and twenty and the second son of Lord Cunningham. He is kind and gentle. A man of study. Timothy will intrude upon your life the least. Never will he chastise you for going about with bare feet. Nor will he expect you to change for meals. Knowing your temperament, I wanted to send you one man who would not seek to change you. But weigh your decision. Timothy will not take command of you, but he will also not take command of your people. Never could he be a formidable laird, which will not go unnoticed by the MacLeod.*

*My dear, Alex, I have no wish to see your fiery spirit smothered, or for you to be placed under the thumb of any man, including myself, which is why I have sent you a selection of suitors so that the choice in the end is yours. Go through each one and choose wisely. Given the vast MacKenzie lands, wealth, and not to mention your fine qualities too numerous to list on this page, I do not doubt if you were to make your intentions known to any one of them that they would immediately see the benefits to the match.*

*Now it is especially important that you understand none of them know my true motive for sending them north to your lands. They believe they are there to offer guidance to you and your warriors in the absence of a chieftain. If they knew they were being appraised like horseflesh at market, they might take offense. Guard this secret well. Also, and equally as important, I have sent another man to you, Rory MacVie. He is NOT one of the men I have put forth as a potential husband. I have sent him to aid you in moving the weapons you have hidden away. This is the only capacity in which Rory is to avail himself to you. He is a great many things and a great man, but he is not the sort of man a respectable lass marries. Beyond that, he possesses no title or wealth. He and his brothers are all agents working as you have for me and the bishop, but recent events have brought attention to the MacVie name. I fear it will not be long before all the MacVie brothers will be forced into hiding or face the Tower. I love Rory as I would a son, but frankly, my child, he is a rake. Heed my words and hold fast to your heart.*

*Regarding the weapons, you and Rory must decide the best time and method to move them. Regarding your selection of husband, you have one month to decide. You can expect my visit in thirty days. If ye permit me, I will attend your wedding in your father's stead. I look forward to that day.*

*You are in my heart and my prayers,*

*A.M.*

Alex focused on steadying her breathing to not reveal how nervous the abbot's letter had made her. Her heart pounded in her ears while she unhurriedly folded the parchment. Then she dropped her hands to her side, taking on a relaxed stance. Long ago, she had learned to mask her nerves in any situation. Still, three men, three strangers, stood before her while, unbeknownst to them, she would be trying them on over the next month like a pair of slippers at market to see how they fit.

And then there was Rory.

She could feel his presence, the weight of his gaze. It had been some time ago when she had requested Abbot Matthew send north another agent to help her move her stockpile of weapons. It was too great an undertaking to accomplish alone, and it would be a relief to have the job done. A shiver coursed up her spine as she thought of completing another mission with Rory. But then she remembered Abbot Matthew's words she had only just read...He is NOT one of the men I have put forth as a potential husband.

She cleared her throat and stepped forward. Her duty was to her clan, and she would not lose sight of that. Clan MacKenzie needed a chieftain. She quickly scanned the three noblemen who stood by patiently awaiting introductions. One of the three would—hopefully—be that chieftain. She smiled and dipped into a low curtsy.

One of the men with chestnut brown hair, deep-set green eyes, and full, appealing lips stepped forward. He dipped his head to her and took her hand, bringing it to those full lips.

"My name is Sir Adam Lennox. I am so terribly sorry for yer loss, Lady Alexandria. I hope my presence here will provide ye comfort. Please know that I am at yer service."

Adam was certainly tall and broad of shoulder and rather handsome. His sympathy seemed genuine. She had also felt his calloused palm when he took her hand and remembered Abbot Matthew's description of Adam as a seasoned knight. His skill in battle would certainly be an asset to the clan.

With another dip of his head, Adam stepped back. Alex shifted her eyes to the next man who came forward.

"I am Sir Robert Gow," he said, bowing low before kissing her hand.

Robert was almost angelic in appearance. He had hair as blond as hers and very dark blue eyes. Two dimples appeared in his cheeks when he smiled, framing white, even teeth. "I'm honored to be chosen by the abbot to assist ye in any way I can." Then he gestured toward the castle stables, the entrance to which was on the other end of the courtyard. "I have been observing some of the comings and goings at yer stables, and I'm already impressed with the MacKenzie horses."

"Thank you," she said, remembering Abbot Matthew had mentioned that Robert knew something of horse breeding. He was certainly handsome, even more so than Adam, but his countenance seemed lighter, less serious, which she also liked.

She could imagine Robert having a playful side, which she knew the children of the MacKenzie clan would enjoy in a chieftain.

Timothy was the last to step forward, and she liked him instantly. He introduced himself simply, using only his given name and leaving off titles.

"My condolences, my lady," he said, clasping her hand in both of his. The compassion she saw in his eyes rang true. "I would be honored to pray with ye and help ye through this trying time."

Timothy was sincere. His eyes radiated warmth and kindness. Unlike either Adam or Robert, his clothing was simple—not unlike her own. Aye, she understood why the abbot had sent Timothy. He would be a servant to the MacKenzie clan, not a lord.

Michael came forward then and gestured to Rory. "I did not hear whether ye made introductions earlier when he was helping ye to yer feet. May I present, Rory MacVie."

A half smile curved Rory's lips, lips she had boldly tasted beneath the cover of darkness, under a canopy of stars. He took her hand and pressed those same lips to her skin. "'Tis a pleasure to meet ye...for the very first time," he said, giving her a knowing smile.

Her heart raced. "The pleasure is mine...for the very first time."

She gently tugged her hand free and stepped away from Rory, trying to escape the pull he had on her senses. She stepped farther back and once more quickly scanned the men standing in front of her, all looking at her expectantly. Then she cleared her throat. "'Tis time for the noon meal. Shall we retire to the keep?" she said, before turning on her heel and heading toward the great hall. Behind her she knew they all followed. Adam, Robert, Timothy...Rory.

Her stomach flipped and her heart pounded. When she had written the abbot, she never would have imagined his solution would be to send her multiple suitors. A new secret mission had begun: one that ended with her choosing a husband. She glanced back at the unknowing suitors, feeling devious and delicious all at the same time.

# Chapter Eight

Rory stepped through the wide arched entrance into Luthmore Castle's great hall. His eyes flitted from the intricately designed tapestries to the massive hearth to the rows of trestle tables filled with villagers enjoying the noon meal. A hum of voices and laughter lent the room a joyful air. Rory had never been in a castle before. He looked up. The ceiling was so high, it may as well have been the sky, with candles flickering around large, iron candelabra like stars. Underfoot, fresh rushes shifted, releasing fragrant lavender into the air, which mingled with the scent of cooked meats, herbs and the smell of freshly baked bread. He smiled, enjoying the lively space. To him it felt like a busy marketplace or village green enclosed within a vast stone belly. He patted his own stomach as it growled in response to the rich aromas.

"Do ye approve?"

Rory's gaze shifted from the high dais where mounted on the wall was the MacKenzie coat of arms, to find Alex looking at him expectantly. Her keen eyes met his with uncharacteristic boldness for a woman—not the haughty entitlement of a noblewoman or that of wanton desire or even defiance. She seemed to move through life with a quiet confidence that so often escaped the fairer sex. To her, she was his equal, the same. He imagined she spoke to all men and women without deference for gender or title, her behavior unaltered whether they appreciated her candor or not.

"I do approve, although I do not believe my approval matters to ye, nor anyone's for that matter."

Her head slanted just slightly to the side as she considered him. "Do ye fashion yer actions or ideals with someone else's approval in mind?"

He smiled, then slowly shook his head. "Nay," he said simply.

"Well, neither do I," she replied and continued to hold his gaze, both at ease just looking at the other.

At length, she cleared her throat. Then her eyes darted toward Michael and the other men who were not three strides away. "Allow me to show ye our tapestries," she said loudly, leading him away from the group. Pointing to a large woven scene with knights on horseback charging at an unseen enemy, she began in a louder voice, "This one is over three hundred years old..." Her voice trailed off as they finished crossing the hall.

"I never thought I would see ye again. Least of all here," she said, still gesturing at the wall as if pointing out the intricacies of the design.

"Trust me," Rory said his voice hushed. "When we first met, this is not where I thought ye'd come from." He motioned toward the full trestle tables and high dais.

Alex shrugged. "'Tis a fair assumption on yer part. Women are scarce in our movement—ladies, well, we are non-existent. I believe I am the only one. But now I'm making assumptions of my own. 'Tis entirely possible that the good abbot has legions of ladies secretly at work."

Rory smiled. "And all wearing tunics lined with silver marks and kissing fellow Scottish rebels in the woods."

Her lips curved in the slightest of smiles. "Mayhap."

"I have not forgotten that kiss."

"Nor have I."

It felt like a continuous bolt of lightning shot off her and straight into his core, igniting currents of need without end. His breathing sped up, becoming shallower, and the sound of her rapid breaths met his ears, further fueling his own desire.

"Enough," she snapped, he knew as much to herself as to him.

He stepped to the side to try to sever the intensity of their attraction. Clearing his throat, he sought to change the subject and made a sweeping motion with his hand meant to encompass the whole of the great hall. "In truth, I'm in awe. Unlike the men in my company, I am but the humble son of a shipyard laborer. I have never set foot in so grand a home."

She laughed. "I've never heard Luthmore Castle referred to as a home, but it certainly is that to me." She also took a step to the side, distancing herself even more. Then she cleared her own throat. "So, what is yer home like?"

"These days I find my rest in a wooded glen or a room at an inn in the latest village to which the Abbot has sent me. But I grew up in Berwick when it was still a Scottish city. My parents, four brothers, and two sisters shared a room not much larger than three of yer trestle tables pushed together."

A shadow of concern reshaped her countenance, drawing her lovely brows together and sharpening her violet eyes. "Ye were in Berwick when it was attacked?"

"Aye." Images of narrow cobbled streets piled high with rotting corpses of men, women, and children flooded his mind, despite his wish not to see them again. He shook his head, chasing away the images.

She drew closer. "Forgive me. I see it pains ye to speak of it."

"It does," he said softly. He closed his eyes and drew a steady breath before once more meeting her eyes. "Most days it is impossible to understand or even believe it happened. I was not there, in the city, when King Edward and his tens of thousands attacked. I had accompanied my sister into the wood that morning to forage for herbs. I am not tortured by the screams of the dying like my brother, Alec, who was in the city that day—one of the few within the city limits to escape the sword and the torch. But I saw its aftermath. I saw the thousands and thousands who were slain. I saw the bodies of my parents and our youngest sister, Rosalyn."

Her hand darted to her face, swiping at her eyes.

"Nay, Alex. Do not cry. So many tears have already been shed. I ken yer own heart suffers the loss of yer father. I did not mean to pile my own grief onto yer already heavy heart."

"Those must have been dark days indeed."

He nodded. "They were. We were exiled of course, my brothers and sister and me. But then we met the abbot, and he brought us into the cause, giving me a direction for my fury and grief. Early on I craved vengeance."

"And now?" she asked.

"Only justice."

She grew quiet and stared at the tapestry, although Rory could tell it was not the colors and pattern she observed but some distant heartache. "Grief and fury also led me to the cause."

He was about to ask her more, but she turned then, her shoulders straight and her face stern with resolve. "Which brings us to the matter at hand. We have a mission."

He would not press her to speak of her pain. Instead, he nodded. "Indeed, we do."

"Meet me in my solar following the evening meal. The guards will grant ye entry. Now, we should return to our company, or tongues will start to wag."

He followed her away from the periphery of the great hall into the joyous fray, passing tables of clan folk who called out in greeting to their lady, but they never used her rightful title. She was not Lady Alexandria to her people; she was just Alex. Rory drank in the noble sight of her. Never had he observed a woman more deserving of the title Lady, even though her hair was still tangled, her dress soiled, her filthy toes peeking out from beneath the hem of her dress. Her nobility was in her bearing. It was in the warmth that radiated from her eyes as she smiled and greeted her people. It was in the humble way she received their good wishes and praise. She was the lady of legends.

He continued to follow her as they made their way past the final row of long wooden tables, but as she continued toward the high dais, he hesitated. At the high table sat a richly dressed young woman. Her was back ramrod straight, and her head was demurely contained by a wimple and veils. On one side of her sat Alex's brother, Will, who looked as polished as a new penny in a velvet tunic. Though when he looked up and smiled at Rory, his face was still dirt-smeared, and his hair stood on end.

Rory smiled and looked past Will to where his traveling companions and the steward of Luthmore Castle stood. Clearly, they were awaiting the arrival of the lady of the keep before they would sit down themselves. Rory was not one of them, nor had he ever wanted to be. He looked at the people who surrounded him with their easy smiles, simple tunics, and relaxed postures. This is where he belonged. He found a free seat at the end of one of the tables and sat down, greeting those around him. Ravenous, he reached into one of the trenchers in the center of the table and grabbed a piece of meat. His fingers dripping with gravy, he groaned in response to the delectable flavor.

Alex smiled at her waiting guests as she mounted the steps to the high table. Then she looked over at Mary, whose eyes lit up as she drew closer. Alex bit the side of her cheek to keep from smiling at her cousin who she knew was bursting beneath her smooth, calm facade. The arrival of four handsome lowlanders had not escaped Mary's notice, and she was clearly dying to ask Alex who they were and why they were there.

Alex cleared her throat, keeping her own excitement in check. Then she glanced back to point Rory to one of the chairs, but she faltered. He was gone. She paused and gazed out over the hall, finding him at one of the long tables, his shirtsleeves rolled up, his elbows on the table while he bit the meat off a bone and laughed at some jest from Corc who sat next to him. It was not hard to hide her disappointment. Her years as an agent to the cause had honed her skills of concealment, but she felt his absence in a way that surprised her. She proceeded forward and dipped in a low curtsy in front of Michael, Adam, Robert, and Timothy.

"Forgive my delay," she said.

Adam came forward then and bowed at the waist. "There is no grievance to forgive, my lady. Do not hurry dinner on our account. We will happily continue to wait while ye change."

"Change?" she said. Then she looked down at her tunic. It was one of two that she alternated every day. She brushed at some of the dust, revealing a patch of Flemish wool dyed to match the heather. It was actually her favorite of the two. Over the years, it had softened and felt like a gentle, warm breeze on her skin. Alex's thoughts returned to Abbot Matthew's letter. Clearly, Adam expected her to behave like a 'proper' lady. One mark against Adam.

Michael cleared his throat and gave her a pointed look. She knew the direction of his thoughts. No doubt he wanted her to take Adam's advice, hurry up to her chambers and pull on her finery so that she looked more like Mary, but that was no surprise. Ever since she was a wee lass running barefoot across the moors, Michael was always trying to persuade Alex to behave in a more ladylike manner. In her own defense, she had always argued that she was a proper lady—she cared for her clan—with her own back and her own sweat and tears. Over the years, she had met several gently born ladies who thought more of their own comfort than the wellbeing of their people. Typically decisive, she suddenly found herself in a quandary. The only times she had changed for meals was the rare occasion she found herself the guest in someone else's fortress. But then she looked at her father's empty chair. Her clan needed a chieftain. She curtsied again and was about to turn on her heel and slip behind the screen to the stairwell that would lead to her chambers, where she might dig a piece of finery out from a dusty trunk, when her stomach growled loudly. This was ridiculous. She could not wait dinner any longer.

"I'm afraid I am famished," she said, directing her comment to Adam.

He smiled, gently conceding. "Then let us feast."

She smiled in return. At least he hadn't pushed the point. She held out her hand for him to escort her to the table, but Robert cut in front of him, beating him to the job.

"My lady," Robert said in greeting. "Allow me."

She craned her neck to meet his lively blue eyes. He really was incredibly tall and more handsome even than she first judged him to be. More than that, he possessed such a joyful countenance. Hmmm...one mark for Robert.

She took the seat next to the chieftain's chair while Robert claimed the chair next to hers. Adam respectfully moved past her father's chair and William's and sat on the other side of Mary. Timothy sat down next to Michael on the far end of the high table.

A moment later, a young woman stepped over and filled their cups. "Thank ye, Fenella."

"Yer most welcome," she said, bobbing in a quick curtsy.

Following just after Fenella, several servants arrived bearing trenchers of meats and bread.

"Tell me of yer family, Robert," Alex said, reaching for a piece of meat.

"'Tis good of ye to ask, my lady. My father is a horse breeder. In fact, my family's horses are celebrated throughout Scotland and England and even across the water in France."

"Really? Is there a secret to yer family's success?" she asked.

"Indeed there is, and it is one I do not mind imparting to anyone willing to listen. The Gow family looks to our horses as extended members of our family."

This confession warmed Alex's heart. "I have always loved animals as well."

"I'm so happy to hear ye say that," Robert said agreeably. "Then ye will understand that occasionally I've even taken to one of the geldings as if I were its mum. Well, not its real mum, obviously, but a close second, like its Godmum."

Her hand froze, the bread almost to her lips. She cast Robert a sidelong look. "Ye've been a Godmum to a horse?"

He smiled. "'Tis strange I know, but true all the same. At least my feelings have been true."

She cleared her throat, trying to squelch the chuckle looking for a way out. She reached for her cup and took a long sip, dousing her amusement. When she felt composed, she placed the cup down, ready to continue their conversation. "Now that ye mention it, in his letter the abbot did say that ye were something of a horse expert."

Robert blushed ever so slightly, shaking his head.

Well, he wasn't arrogant. Another mark for Robert, although he had just said he was a horse's Godmum. Hmmm...she would have to think on that one.

"I'm certainly not an expert," he said.

"Ye're not?" she said, surprised.

He shook his head even more vehemently. "Dear me, nay. I don't believe anyone could truly claim to be a horse expert. One could spend their whole life studying horses, and still one would learn something new every day. I would be better described as having a passion for horses."

Well, there was nothing wrong with that, she decided. "I have an interest in horses as well," she said.

His face brightened. "Really? Well, did ye know that horses are ticklish?"

This time she could not contain her laughter. Surely, he jested. But his face grew increasingly serious, and she realized that he was speaking in earnest.

Smothering her laughter, she adopted a serious tone, "Nay, I was not aware of that."

He smiled, clearly happy to enlighten her. "Indeed, they are, and in truth, ye've always known this."

She cocked a brow at him. "I have?"

"Aye, ye've just not put the pieces together."

Biting her cheek to contain her smile, she managed to say, "I'm sure ye're going to solve this puzzle for me right now."

"Most willingly," he said. "Ye see, horses shudder to shake flies off their backs, which means their hides must be sensitive to the itch and annoyance of the flies' little legs."

"But what does that have to do with tickling? When I think of tickling, I think of the sort that produces laughter."

Robert crunched his fingers and touched the top of her hand with fast feather-light flicks of his fingertips. "But cannot tickling also be an irritant?"

"I can think of other things that are much more irritating," she said dryly, withdrawing her hand from his touch and placing it on her lap. "I need more wine," she said, gesturing to Fenella who stood in wait with the jug. After she refilled their cups, Alex gestured to the seat next to Robert's. "Fenella, please join us." Then she said to Robert. "Fenella loves horses."

Robert smiled in greeting and soon the two were conversing easily, allowing Alex a moment's peace. Sitting back in her chair, she took another sip of wine while she considered her sampling of men. So far, she had learned little of Adam, other than he was handsome, evidently a very skilled knight, and favored social conventions. He seemed to be in possession of several admiral qualities, but he was bound to find certain aspects of her character wanting.

Girlish laughter erupted from the trestle table where Rory sat, drawing her gaze. Corc had slid farther down the bench. Now, bright-eyed lassies surrounded him. They were all leaning close, clearly hanging on his every word.

She forced herself to look away. She had clan business to consider. After all, they needed a laird. Her eyes darted to Rory again, but she shook her head against the direction of her thoughts.

A laird of noble birth.

Her fingers gripped her cup tighter. Where was she? Oh, aye, then there was Robert. Robert had winsome looks and a cheerful disposition...but...could she tolerate a lifetime of odd horse talk?

This time it was a rich masculine laugh that pulled her attention back to Rory and his gaggle of love-struck MacKenzie lassies. Alison, Helen's youngest and still unmarried sister who was not known for her good sense, was leaning close to Rory, whispering something in his ear.

Still, Rory and Alison's conversation was none of her affair. Clan MacKenzie needed a laird of noble birth, not a man as alluring and forbidden as Rory. She clenched her fists against the weakness of her own thoughts.

All right, back to business. She leaned forward, looking past Mary, Adam, and Michael to where Timothy sat. He and Michael were engaged in what looked like sensible and serious conversation.

Hmmm...mayhap Timothy was the one. He appeared level-headed and cared nothing for useless conventions. Even Abbot Matthew had said that Timothy was the man who would accept her for who she really was.

Suddenly, less than jovial feminine voices drew her attention. Alison and another lass were now squabbling for the seat closest to Rory.

"Right," Alex said under her breath and placed her hands on the table, coming to her feet.

The men at the high table began to push back their chairs to stand as a courtesy to her. "Nay, gentlemen, please keep yer seats." She walked the length of the table and leaned next to Michael.

"We have been remiss," she whispered in Michael's ear. "One of our guests has not joined our company at the high table."

Michael looked across the room, following the direction of her gaze. "He is a peasant," he said under his breath.

"He would not be the first peasant to grace this table. Look. Fenella is sitting at the end there speaking to Robert. William is not truly of noble birth."

Michael flattened his hands on the table. "Fine," he whispered. "I will go and bring him to our table, although he looks rather comfortable where he is."

Alex looked across the room to where Rory sat. He looked too comfortable. She knew she couldn't have him, but she certainly wasn't going to let another MacKenzie woman have him either. Moments later, while Michael and Rory approached the high dais, she looked for empty chairs. There was one chair free at the very end of the table next to Timothy or there was the chair next to hers, her father's chair. In that moment, she wanted nothing more than for him to fill the chieftain's seat, but she resisted the baser commands of her body and allowed Michael to lead Rory to the last chair.

She leaned forward to see past the line of faces separating them and raised her cup. A warm smile lifted his full lips and set her heart to racing. She quickly leaned back to escape the sinful sight of him. She had to keep her eyes on the true prize, on what mattered most—the wellbeing of her people. More than anything, they needed a laird, and as much as she wanted Rory, hungered for him, the peasant son of a dockhand could not be the one. It would be a direct insult to the MacLeod, which would endanger her people. She drained her wine and sat back, noticing that the table of MacKenzie lassies was silently eying Rory, however, now from a safe distance.

Go ahead and look all ye want, lassies. How could she blame them? Rory was the kind of man that could bring even the most chaste of women to their knees.

# Chapter Nine

After nightfall when the great hall was quiet, Rory disappeared behind the screen and followed Alex's directions to her solar. Two large warriors stood guard at the door. Rory eyed their battle-hardened physiques, which were naked to the eye in the simple plaids they wore. Typically, when there was a guarded room to which he needed to gain access, he sought entry only after days, sometimes weeks, of planning, and never without the support other agents. Instinct bade him find another way into the room or arm himself for battle, but Alex had assured him that the guards would let him pass.

Well...there was a first for everything.

He strode purposefully toward the guards, wearing a friendly smile on his face.

"Good evening, Rory MacVie," the guard on the left said.

Rory paused for an instant but quickly recovered from his initial surprise at hearing his name spoken. "Good evening," he began. "I am meant to—"

"We ken," the guard on the right said. "Ye're here to meet with Alex. She's already told us." He opened the door and motioned for Rory to enter. "She said to make yerself comfortable, and that she'll be along shortly."

"Ye have my thanks," Rory said as he stepped into the room. The door closed behind him. He stood for a moment, taking in his surroundings. A small fire smoldered in the hearth on the right side of the room. Facing the orange embers were two high-backed, ornately carved chairs. Above the mantle was a painting of a woman with fierce, dark eyes and hair so fair the artist's brush made it as white as the moon that shone in the upper corner of the canvas. The woman exuded grace and power. Rory stepped closer and considered the eyes of the subject. She stared back as if life pulsed in her painted veins.

Tearing himself away, he forced his feet to walk farther into the room. There was a large desk, littered with parchment. Several rocks clearly painted by children tamed the papers with their weight. He drew closer, drawn to the images of wee handprints and flowers. Just then a gust of wind blew, and a piece of parchment not weighed down lifted and zig-zagged in a slow dance to the floor. Rory bent over and picked up the page. He set it down and started to walk away, but from the corner of his eye he read his name. He splayed his hands wide on either side of the letter and began to read.

*My Dearest Alexandria,*

*My heart is heavy as I too grieve for your father. As you know, Donnan was my dearest friend from youth. Never has there lived a kinder or more generous man. Take comfort knowing that he now sits with our Lord at His table. Also, please know that you are not alone. I received your letter and am fully prepared to guide you in finding a husband. Marriage is a sound choice at this time. To this end, I have sent you a selection of men, three in number.*

"So, Abbot Matthew is playing matchmaker," he said aloud, shaking his head in amazement. He should have guessed there was an ulterior motive sending the unmarried, young, generally pleasant noblemen north. "As if any of them could handle a woman like Alexandria," he scoffed.

A nag of suspicion crept up his back. If the abbot had set aside his vows long enough to lie to Adam, Robert, and Timothy, had he also lied to Rory? "What is my true reason for being here?" he said, skimming the letter.

"What the blazes," he cursed, straightening and seizing the letter in his hands.

*I have sent another man to you, Rory MacVie. He is NOT one of the men I have put forth as a potential husband. I have sent him to aid you in moving the weapons you have hidden away. This is the only capacity to which Rory is to avail himself to you. He is a great many things and a great man, but he is not the sort of man a respectable lass marries.*

"So, that is how it is to be, Abbot Matthew," he said, scowling. His head jerked up. He looked hard at the door. Alex had just called out to her men in greeting. He placed the letter down before silently crossing to the fire and quickly sitting in one of the high-backed chairs just as the door swung open.

"Good evening, Rory," she said, moving confidently into the room. "Forgive my delay. I was going over tomorrow's menu with Jean."

Rory's mind raced. He was torn by being offended by the abbot's words or accepting some blame for the monk's frank assessment of Rory's past—not that Rory considered himself a rake. He was never dishonest with women. He did not feign affection or make false promises to fill his bed. Certainly, he enjoyed women and had never apologized for that, but he also had never met one who could lay claim to his heart. That being said, if his sister Rose ever strutted around with a man like himself, he would beat the blackguard to the ground. In the end, he supposed it was fair of the abbot to not recommend Rory to Alex as a potential suitor. And by God, he had no interest in being laird. Adam, Robert, or Timothy were all more suitable choices. Still, if that was true, why in God's name did he feel like beating the living hell out of all three of them?

"I hope ye've not been waiting long," she said, sitting down in the chair beside his.

Rory shrugged. "I've been comfortable enough." Then he gestured to the painting of the woman above the mantle. "She caught my eye straightaway. 'Tis a powerful portrait."

"'Tis of my mother, painted by my father."

Rory stared hard at the woman in the painting. Tangled white-blond hair whipped around her sharp features. There was so much passion within her painted eyes, he almost believed she could see straight into his soul. "Ye take after her. I see ye in her coloring and her manner."

"Ye're half right. I do have my mother's coloring, but that is where the commonalities end, at least in terms of appearance. She was quiet and very refined, every bit the proper lady, but a fire blazed deep within her. It was the fire my father hoped to capture. He said he had painted her inside-out."

Rory continued to study the portrait, trying to keep his thoughts from returning to the abbot's letter.

"I've given a great deal of thought to our latest mission," Alex said.

He released a slow, even breath, happy to be distracted by the mission at hand, which did at least appear to be the true reason the abbot had sent him north. He would have time to make sense of the rest of the letter later.

"It will take a full day to gather the weapons. There are some axes and targs but mostly swords, hundreds actually."

Rory's brows lifted. "Ye've managed to amass an armory's worth of weapons on yer own?"

A sad smile curved her lips. "I did not do this on my own."

"Nay?" he said, sitting straighter. "I did not realize there were others privy to our cause here."

"There are none here at Luthmore. It is important for the sake of my people that no one ever connects me to the cause." She stared off into the fire. "What would become of them?" Then she turned her head and once more they locked eyes. "'Tis my greatest fear, Rory. That somehow I will be implicated, and my people made to suffer for my actions."

Rory leaned forward and covered her hand with his. He couldn't help it. Seeing her wrinkle her brow with worry instantly made him want to reach out to her, hold her, protect her, especially since her fears were warranted. If her identity were ever revealed, her entire clan would feel King Edward's wrath.

She turned her hand over so that her palm now pressed into his. He felt the pulse in her wrist quicken and forgot all about her worry. She leaned closer to him, her tongue darting out to lick her lips. His eyes dropped to her full, glistening mouth. He leaned toward her, hungry for those parted lips. "God's blood," he cursed aloud the same instant she jerked her hand away as though his touch had burned her. Both breathless, they stared at each other.

"Ye stay over there," she said, motioning to his chair. Then she waved her hands in a panic near her chair. "This is my space." Then she waved her hands to encompass his chair. "That is yer space."

Rory gripped the arms of his chair. "Got it."

After the pounding of his heart began to subside, he cleared his throat. "Now then, back to the mission."

"Aye," she nodded, she too gripping the arms of the chair. "The mission."

"Who, may I ask, helped ye gather the weapons?"

The tension fled her body, and the impassioned composition of her face was replaced by sadness. "Lord Robin Campbell."

"Lord Robin?" Rory said, surprised.

She looked at him curiously. "Ye knew him?"

"Aye, I did. I worked with him on several occasions. He was a hero among the agents. Everyone grieved when we learned he fell at Dunbar." He paused, taking in her obvious hurt. "He was important to ye?" Rory asked softly.

She nodded, her eyes welling with tears the instant before she turned away to look into the flames. "He was my father's closest friend," she said, her voice barely above a whisper. "And my betrothed."

Rory's mouth filled with the bitter taste of loss. He was acutely aware of the pain she suffered.

"I dream about him still," she said. "Always in my dreams he dies slowly, painfully." She swiped at the tears trailing down her cheeks. "Ye can't imagine how often I've thought of his last moments."

He released a slow breath to hold his own emotions in check. "I do ken," he said. "Every day I wonder about what sort of end my parents and sister faced. Every day I pray they did not suffer."

She wiped her eyes and showed him her tear-streaked palms. "This is the reason I risk so much for the cause. What else am I to do with all this pain?"

He nodded his accord. "'Tis the same for all of Scotland's agents. We risk our freedom, our lives to save others from the same pain."

They sat in silence for several moments. Then at length she said, "I admired Robin with all my heart. He was a compassionate leader."

"That I do not doubt," Rory said. Then he remembered the abbot's letter. "Lord Robin passed away three years ago. Should yer father not have found ye another husband?"

"Aye," she said. "But he was ill, so terribly ill. We feared that if anyone knew just how infirm he truly was, that greed would turn our neighbors against us. So, we hid the extent of his suffering." She swiped again at her eyes, whisking away the last evidence of her grief. "But my clan is without a chieftain, something I intend to remedy very soon." Abruptly coming to her feet, she looked down at him. "Walk with me."

He stood and followed her out of the room and up a winding stairwell that led to the battlements. Once outside, they both breathed the fresh night air.

Suddenly she turned and narrowed her eyes on him. "How long have ye known Adam?"

He shrugged. "Just since our journey north to yer home." Then he grinned. "As a commoner and rebel, I do not encounter nobility unless I'm in the process of robbing them blind to give to the cause."

Her face brightened. "Aye, ye're one of the Saints. I've admired yer work. In fact, I've always longed to ride with ye. Mayhap, one day yer brothers will take on a sixth rider."

Rory shook his head. "I fear the Saints are no more. My brother Jack is on the run from King Edward's knights. Last

I knew, he and my youngest brother, Ian, and my sister, Rose, were heading to the Isle of Colonsay."

"What of yer other brothers?"

"Last I knew, Quinn was on a mission to save an English lady. And Alec...well...I really can't say. I haven't seen or heard from him in months. He is an agent like us. I can only assume he, too, is on a mission." His eyes narrowed on her. "How did ye know about the Saints in the first place?"

"Abbot Matthew has told me about ye and yer brothers."

Rory laughed and shook his head. "For a man sworn to keep secrets, the abbot's tongue has the capacity to wag."

"Nay, I believe he is the picture of discretion. I just think he could not help but brag about his Saints. He loves ye, ye know. And the rest of yer brothers."

Rory thought about the less than flattering words Abbot Matthew had written in his letter and for a flash of an instant he doubted the abbot's affection. But then he broadened his thinking and considered Alex. It was clear Abbot Matthew also held her dear to his heart. He could not blame the abbot for not considering Rory as a suitor. Not only was he without title, wealth, or connection, he had behaved as a man with a fickle heart.

She turned from him and stared out over the battlements. "On the road north, what sort of man did Adam strike ye as?" she asked, a forced casualness to her tone.

Rory resisted the urge to scowl. She was fishing for more information about her suitors. Well, he understood why he was not in the running to be her husband nor did he care to be. Not that he wouldn't have wished to court Alex; he just wasn't meant to be a laird. He paused then and looked at her lovely profile, the strength in her stance. He had offered her his hand earlier when they first stepped out onto the battlements. Her palms had been nearly as calloused as his—God's blood, she was magnificent. He raked his hand through his hair. Fine. He admired her and wanted her so badly it hurt. This he couldn't deny. And although he could never be laird of the MacKenzie, he was not going to recommend another man to the job.

"He's the kind of man who snores," he bit out.

She raised a brow. "He snores? This is what ye have to say about Adam?"

"Aye, and loudly." Then he decided to change the subject as far away from Adam as possible. "When do we gather the weapons?"

"Aye, back to the plan," she said approvingly. "I don't know how we got so far off the subject."

He wanted to accuse her of being distracted by the pretty faces of her new suitors, but remembered that was un-fair—Alex had to marry. She had no choice. Her clan depended on her acting wisely and quickly. The sooner they completed their mission and he returned south, the better for her. "Why wait?" he said. "Let's go tomorrow."

"All right. Tomorrow it is," she agreed. "Leave the keep early in the morning and meet me in the village at Corc's cottage. I will join ye there after Mass."

"The old man I sat with at dinner?"

She nodded. "The same."

He took her calloused hand in his and pressed a kiss to her roughened skin. "Until tomorrow." Then he turned on his heel and hurried away from her before he pledged to wed her him-self and protect her people with his life if need be.

# Chapter Ten

Alex collapsed on her bed, burying her face in her pillow. "I do not ken what to do," she groaned, her voice muffled.

"To me, the choice is clear," Mary said.

Alex sat up and looked at her cousin, who was sitting on the end of the bed in a white, silk nightdress. "Sir Adam Lennox is the one." Mary leaned closer, her brown eyes sparkling. "I had the fine pleasure of conversing with him during dinner, and he was everything a gentleman should be—intelligent, well-mannered, solicitous. He spoke well of his family. His elder sister sounds enchanting." Mary clasped her hands together. "Not to mention, he is handsome, with the most beautiful green eyes I've ever seen."

Alex pursed her lips together before pointing out, "Aye, but he was so clean, even after journeying a fair distance."

Mary threw up her hands. "Is that really so awful?"

"I'm not filling my day with dressing for meals when I could be caring for my people," Alex declared, crossing her arms over her chest.

"If ye want to know, I think Robert is the one," Rosie said, chiming in from her perch on the other side of the bed. "He's right handsome and cheerful." Rosie stared off dreamily while she finished plaiting her waist-length black hair. Like Alex, she was still clad in the same tunic she'd worn that day. Nightclothes were a luxury beyond Rosie's reach. As for Alex, she simply deemed them unnecessary.

Brows drawn, Alex considered Rosie's judgment. "I suppose ye're right, although I believe he is rather strange."

"'Tis too soon to judge any of these men," Mary cautioned. "Robert might be amiable when conditions are right, but what happens when he is provoked? He could be quick to temper."

"The abbot did say that all three men had even temperaments," Alex recalled.

"Robert's a lamb," Rosie gushed. "Ye can tell he'd be gentle in bed by the way he speaks of his horses."

"Rosie," Mary exclaimed, her cheeks turning red.

Alex wrinkled her nose. "Ye don't think he was just a little too excited about his horses?"

"Perhaps his dinner conversation was odd, but do we not all possess a wee dash of strangeness?" Rosie gestured pointedly to Alex's grubby feet.

"If we are going to look honestly at my own oddities, then mayhap Timothy is the best man after all. I believe he would be the most accepting of who I really am," Alex said.

Mary and Rosie exchanged glances.

"What is it?" Alex demanded. "Why not Timothy?"

Both ladies held their silence until at last Rosie sighed. "Och, I'll be the one to say it. Bless Timothy's heart, but he's too soft to be laird."

Mary nodded. "I agree with Rosie."

Alex couldn't dismiss their concern. Timothy was certainly no warrior. She sighed. "Then Mary, ye're right. Clearly, Rory is the one."

Mary and Rosie's brows shot up. "Rory?" they both exclaimed together.

Alex's hand flew to cover her mouth. Then she pulled a blanket over her head.

"Alexandria MacKenzie, come out from under that blanket at once," Mary demanded while yanking on Alex's woolen defense.

"Nay," Alex groaned. "Go away."

"What is all this fuss for?" Alex heard Rosie say. "Rory's devilish good looks are fine, to be sure, but ye read the abbot's letter. He's not one of yer options."

"Alex, ye're hiding something," Mary said, tugging harder on the blanket.

Then Alex heard Mary suck in a sharp breath. "Black hair, the most beautiful sky-blue eyes ever to be seen, wickedly handsome, one of Scotland's agents." Mary gasped.

Alex cringed, burrowing deeper beneath her covers.

"Rory is the agent from the woods," Mary blurted. "The one who undressed ye!"

It was Rosie's turn to gasp. "Alex, is this true?"

Alex sighed and pushed the blanket down. "He is the same."

"Well, it doesn't matter," Mary announced, straightening her spine.

Rosie nodded in agreement. "She's right, Alex. Ye must forget that night."

Alex sat up. "Ye're both right. I ken ye're right." She covered her face with her hands. "'Tis just easier said than done."

At length, she felt a gentle tug on her fingers. Dropping her hands in her lap, she looked into Mary's kind, brown eyes.

"Remember, Alex," Mary said softly. "Remember yer mother's wisdom. The wellbeing of the clan comes first." Then she pressed a kiss to Alex's cheek and scooted off the bed, pulling Rosie by the hand.

"We will leave ye now so that ye might consider the true weight of yer decision," Mary said with Rosie in tow.

"Saints above, what am I to do?" Alex groaned, falling back onto her pillow and once more burying herself beneath her blankets.

ALEX SAT ON A BENCH, gazing out the solar casement at the stretch of village and crops below. The sun hung just above the horizon, painting the world in soft gold.

"Good morrow, cousin."

She turned to see Mary standing in the doorway. She wore a cream-colored fitted wimple, which framed her heart-shaped face. Draped over her head cascaded layers of matching lace veils. Her deep green tunic complimented her lovely brown eyes. Alex stood and crossed the room. "Good morrow," she said, pressing a kiss to Mary's cheek. "Ye look beautiful, cousin."

"As do ye," Mary said, smiling with approval as she eyed Alex's finely embroidered surcote.

Alex spun in a circle. "I thought ye might approve."

"I do, indeed," Mary said, reaching out to smooth the one veil Alex wore to cover her unbound, pale blond hair. "Ye can wear my new silk wimple. The blue would bring out the violet of yer—"

Alex put up her hand. "Ye can stop right there. Yer reminder last night informed my choice of surcote this morning." Alex ran her hands down her waist, skimming the lavender fabric. "'Tis my best as ye well know. And Rosie spent an hour brushing out my hair. But ye'll never get one of those prison cells around my head."

Mary laughed. "I think ye exaggerate, dear cousin. But I'll not push ye. I ken ye're liable to retreat like cornered prey back into one of yer filthy, worn tunics."

"Ye know me so well," Alex said, smiling. "Shall we head down?"

Mary nodded, and together, they descended the stairs into the great hall. Stepping around the screen, they spotted Adam, Timothy, Robert, Michael, and William waiting near the courtyard entrance.

"Behold, yer three suitors," Mary said, under her breath. "Just think how scandalized they would be if they knew we were, at this very moment, judging their stock."

"Nay, they would be offended if they knew that," Alex whispered. "They would be scandalized if they discovered it was Abbot Matthew who sent them to me as studs."

Mary coughed demurely into her handkerchief to conceal her amusement. Then she squeezed Alex's hand. "I still say the competition is over—Adam is the one. Look at how strong and handsome he is," she whispered.

Alex scanned the men, her gaze slowly passing over Adam. "Aye, but what of his heart?" she said quietly. "To us, he has been kind, but we are his equals in station. What I must know is will he be compassionate to those he might view as beneath him."

Mary leaned closer. "One month is hardly time to judge the true character of a man."

"I agree, which is why I've arranged a test."

"What sort of test?" Mary whispered hurriedly, but it was too late. They were almost upon the men.

"Wheest," Alex breathed. "Ye'll see."

"Good morrow, ladies," Michael said, his stare fixed on Alex. "Ye both look especially lovely today."

Alex resisted the urge to roll her eyes. Dressed in her finest attire, she looked every part the proper lady Michael had always nagged her to be.

"Ye're so clean," Will said, eyeing her suspiciously. "I'm almost afraid to hug ye."

She opened her arms wide. "My dear brother, I'm never too dirty or too clean to hug."

He squeezed the breath from her, then wiped his freckled nose on his sleeve. "Do ye mind if I run ahead? I'm meeting wee Calum."

"For Mass?"

"Aye."

She smiled. "Then run along. Mind ye listen to the good father, and ye don't stand there whispering the whole time."

"I promise," Will said before darting from the hall.

Adam stepped forward then, offering both Mary and Alex an arm. "Ye both do, indeed, look lovely."

Alex smiled and placed her hand on Adam's bicep. Hard, muscled contours flexed beneath her fingertips. Clearly, he was a man of action. She gazed up at his profile. His skin, smooth and tan, stretched tautly over high, wide cheekbones. His nose was straight, not misshapen like so many knights she had encountered, and his full lips begged to be kissed. In particular, she admired his chestnut brown hair that gleamed with flecks of gold and red. He turned and looked down at her and smiled, revealing even, white teeth.

Certainly, his looks and intelligence were indisputable, but was he truly kind?

Alex eyed the kitchen entrance into the great hall and smiled when Rosie appeared carrying a basket teeming with dirty linens.

She was about to find out.

"Good morrow," Rosie said as she passed in front of Alex and her guests, but then Rosie stumbled and her basket tumbled to the floor, scattering its contents. Straightaway, Adam released Alex and Mary's arms and bent to help Rosie to her feet. Likewise, Timothy and Robert knelt to the ground alongside Michael to help gather laundry.

Alex backed away, smiling at the men. One mark for them all.

A moment later, Mary joined her, also observing the attentive men and their favorite maid. Alex hid her smile behind her hand when she noticed Rosie thanking Robert overly long, but Robert did not let his greatest admirer down. He bowed at the waist after handing Rosie back her basket, causing Alex's maid to turn as red as a ripe apple.

"That was not like Rosie at all. She's always so efficient and—Wait!" Mary hissed under her breath, turning to face Alex. "That was yer doing, wasn't it?"

Alex smiled and gave a little shrug. "Ye've met yer share of nobility who would not deign to help a commoner. I thought I would test their instincts to gain insight into their hearts."

"Well, they all passed yer test."

"Indeed, they did."

Mary grinned. "Then ye've no argument to make against Adam. He is the one. Alex, he is perfect."

Alex sighed. "He may be the perfect man—but I wonder if the perfect man is right for me. Anyway," she whispered, starting to move away, "Rory said he snores." She hurried forward to escape Mary's next attempt to champion Adam. Then she winked at Rosie who was bobbing down the hall with her basket intact.

"Damnation," Alex cursed under her breath before she smiled and rejoined the men. She had half hoped that two of her three suitors would have stood by while Rosie struggled to gather her linens and get back on her feet, revealing their hearts lacked true compassion. Whichever man then had stepped forward to help would have been the one, making the decision simple. Her test, in the end, proved pointless, which she should have known. Abbot Matthew would never have sent her men whose true goodness was in doubt.

"Will Rory not be joining us for Mass?" Timothy asked.

Alex smiled at Timothy. Of course he would be caring enough to notice their party was incomplete. But only she, Mary, and Rosie knew that Rory awaited her in the village so that they might carry out a secret mission for Scotland.

"Nay," Alex answered. "Corc, a dear, old codger in the village, mentioned to Rory that his roof had sprung a leak, and Rory was kind enough to offer his assistance."

Timothy smiled his approval. "We are closer to God when we help our brothers and sisters."

"Ye're very right," Alex agreed, warmth flooding her heart. Her eyes passed over his simple tunic. "In fact, ye could be just right for me." She had not meant to speak those words aloud.

"To escort me to Mass," she said quickly. Timothy smiled and stepped forward, offering her his arm, which she gladly accepted.

Once in the small chapel, they all stood in a row facing the altar. Adam seemed to follow the Mass with care to every detail. What's more, he sang beautifully. Robert appeared devout and heartfelt, but his voice croaked from his throat like a choking sparrow. Mary looked at Alex, her eyes wide with horror. Alex soundlessly scolded her, although inside she could not help but cringe.

On the walk back to the castle, she decided to take her cousin's advice and spend time with Adam. By all accounts, he would make the best chieftain. But just as she started toward him, Robert intercepted her once again, offering her his arm.

"May I escort ye back to the keep?"

She glanced at Adam and could see his disappointment. Still, she had no choice but to weave her arm through Robert's. "Of course," she said. "Thank ye."

Again, she was struck by Robert's fine looks, finer even than Adam's. Rosie certainly had good reason to admire him. His golden blond hair shone in the sun while his dark blue eyes held warmth and kindness. When he smiled, his whole face lit up. Alex started to reconsider her earlier dismissal of Robert when they passed by the stables. Straightaway, he began telling her about his visit that very morning with the stable master. She tried to steer the conversation in different directions to see if he could inform broader topics—his family, the weather, planning for Lammas, but somehow, he always managed to bring it straight back to horses.

She glanced sidelong at Adam and Mary who were strolling together and laughing at some mutual jest. Then she looked back at Timothy who walked slowly behind them all, his hands clasped in prayer, clearly still conversing with the Holy Father.

For pity's sake, everyone was having a more interesting conversation than she.

The short journey from the chapel across the courtyard and into the great hall felt like an eternity. Once inside, Alex continued to listen while Robert discussed proper horse grooming. But the moment his string of sentences broke, and he paused, she pounced.

"Forgive me, Robert, but I am due to meet the village midwife. She's in need of supplies." Bidding farewell to her company, she dipped in a quick curtsy and hurried from the hall. Once inside her chambers, the others were forgotten. Rosie helped her out of her finery and into her threadbare tunic. Alex sighed as the familiar, soft fabric fell in place.

"Ye just make certain yer clothes stay on this time," Mary admonished as Alex lifted the trap door in her chamber floor and started down the stairs that would lead through a tunnel, which ran beneath the moat and ended on the other side of the outer wall.

"Ye ken he had to undress me last time," Alex shot back over her shoulder.

"Ye ken ye liked it more than ye should have," Rosie countered.

Alex opened her mouth to issue a sharp retort but then stopped herself. With a shrug, she started again down the stairs, unable to argue Rosie's point. She had enjoyed Rory's touch and certainly more than she should have, which is exactly why she had kissed him.

Once beyond the outer wall, she had to stop herself from running through the village as she made her way to Corc's cottage. Giving a light rap on the door, she opened it, immediately locking eyes with Rory. In the same instant, her knees weakened. Her heart started to pound. His sky-blue eyes shone as brightly as his smile, which was wide and heartfelt, the most beautiful smile. Her chest tightened as she continued to stare at him. Saint's above, but she wanted him.

He stood and brought his finger to his full lips to silence her greeting. She noticed then that Corc was asleep on his pallet. Soundlessly, Rory crossed the small room and gently took her arm, both turning to leave when a tickle grazed her neck. A glint of silver on the ground caught her eye. Her necklace had slipped off. She bent to retrieve it the same moment Rory did. A sharp pain shot through her head when it collided with his. She mouthed a silent curse to accompany his string of silent curses. While she still rubbed her pained skull, he bent and picked up her necklace. He found the break in the chain and pinched the metal to re-close the link.

"It broke recently," she explained. "I thought I fixed it, but it still must be faulty."

He stepped closer, facing her. "'Tis beautiful."

His masculine scent teased her nose. She licked her lips as heat gathered in her core. He stepped closer still. She strained to swallow while he threaded his fingers through her hair and swept it over one shoulder, exposing her neck. A ripple of pleasure shot up her spine. Her fingers stiffened straight out, straining to touch him. He leaned his head down, his cheek a breath from hers while he slowly slipped her necklace into place, his fingers grazing her skin. Her breath caught as he leaned closer to see the clasp, his lips brushing her ear, his warm breath caressing her neck, filling her entire body with aching need.

"Oh God," she gasped, pushing past him and charging out into fresh air.

She turned then and looked back at him. A knowing smile curved his sensual lips.

"Come on," she bristled, trying to regain control. "We need a good ride."

"My thoughts exactly," Rory said, the heat in his eyes telling her exactly what kind of ride he meant.

She raked her hand through her hair. "*Alba gu bràth*," she said, her voice laced with desperation. "Let's remember why we're here."

# Chapter Eleven

Alex raced over the moors astride her large, white stallion with her tunic pushed high past her knees. The wind blasted her face, driving back her hair into a tangled white-gold banner. A smile, wide and jubilant, stretched her lips as freedom's intoxicating potency gripped her innately restless being—which she suppressed for the sake of duty, title, and for the people she loved. For at her core, her very heart, she was as wild as the wolf that prowled the night, racing over the moors to satisfy its animal desires. Only during a mission could she release and satiate her true nature. What's more, after the shock of meeting her unexpected, not to mention, oblivious suitors, it felt rapturous to be outside the walls of Luthmore, far from the confines of her looming and life-altering choice.

She glanced back at Rory whose face mirrored her own fervor for the ride. He smiled, bent low over his black mare, giving chase after her horse just for the simple thrill of it. Locking eyes, they both laughed, allowing the exhilaration of their pace and the bright warmth of the day to be their masters. More than that, the excitement of the mission coursed through her veins, and well she knew it lit a fire within him too. Agents were inherently reckless. That was their one absolute commonality—that and their unyielding loyalty to Scotland.

She drove her heels into her horse's flanks and raced toward the distant coastline. Salt imbued the air. She inhaled the scent. The gently sloping moors gave way to increasingly rough and pointed swells, like rocky waves churning a verdant sea.

And then the green was gone, leaving only jagged rocks that clustered together forming teeming cliffs, beyond which hid the gray-blue water.

"Whoa," she said, bringing her horse to an abrupt halt at the very edge where terrain met air.

Rory eased his horse alongside hers. "Ye were right. I needed that."

She laughed, her face flushed and vibrant from the exercise. He leaned toward her in his saddle and swept tangled flaxen strands of soft hair from her eyes.

"I'm good at guessing people's needs," she said. Then she turned away, nudging her horse forward to walk alongside the cliff edge. "Follow me, but don't look down."

Not heeding her own advice, Alex leaned over to peek at the churning waves crashing against the sheer rock face. She leaned farther still. Then a flash of silver caught his eye. His hand shot out, but it was too late.

"My necklace," she said, clutching her bare throat.

He swung down from his horse and peered over the edge. Her necklace had landed on a wide, flat rock protruding several feet down the side of the cliff. Without hesitation, he crouched on his heels and lowered himself over the edge, his fingers straining to hold his weight. Ridges in the wall allowed the narrowest shelf for his toes. He tightened his core, climbing down until he was alongside the necklace. Releasing one hand, his fingers snaked out, snagging the chain before quickly returning to grip the wall. He looked up to find her peering down at him. She stared hard, her body unmoving. He grunted, pulling himself up, all the while his eyes never leaving hers. He found the surface and hauled himself to the top, every muscle in his body straining against the constant downward force. A moment later he stood, hands on his knees, catching his breath.

"What were ye thinking?" she demanded.

He ignored her question and removed her charm from the silver chain, which he stashed in his saddlebag for safe keeping.

Then he reached behind his own neck and untied the strip of leather he wore, from which hung a small, silver cross. He added her charm to the strip before turning to face her. "May I?" he said gently. Her eyes flashed at him; clearly an admonishment sat just on the tip of her tongue, but she refrained and turned her back to him.

Warmth flooded up her spine as once more she felt his fingertips brush her skin. His hot breath fell on her neck while he tied the string with her beloved trinity knot now nestled beside his silver cross. She closed her eyes, savoring the feel of him, the heat of his body pressed so closely to hers. "Ye're a reckless knave," she whispered, a languid feeling claiming her limbs as she leaned into him. "Ye just risked yer life for my necklace."

"Nay," he whispered in her ear, his lips brushing her skin. "I just risked my life for ye."

"Ye're mad is what ye are." She cleared her throat, trying once again to focus on anything other than her pounding heart. Stepping away, she turned and faced him. "I am grateful. It was a gift from my mother and is sacred to me. Still, it is not worth yer life.

He shrugged. "I've climbed many cliffs."

"But ye could've died."

"I do not fear death," he said simply.

"If ye do not fear death, then what do ye fear?"

"My own cowardice."

She grabbed the reins of her horse and started to walk along the cliff edge, puzzling over his words.

When he joined her, she said, "Ye mean to say ye're afraid of being afraid?"

He nodded.

"That's all?"

Again, he nodded.

Alex shook her head. "I'm not certain I understand."

She saw a slight smile curve his lips just before he shifted his gaze and looked forward. When he spoke next, his voice was unhurried and intimate like an old friend's. "When I was seven years old, I started working the docks with my da. As ships came into port us wee lads would unload the smaller cargo. One time, this lad, Henry, and I grabbed a crate too large for our scrawny arms and dropped it, shattering whatever was inside. A man as big as a giant with cruel eyes grabbed Henry by the back of his tunic and tossed him off the ship, but he couldn't swim. His screams reached my ears. I wanted to jump in after him, but the man grabbed my face hard between his hands and bent at the waist, sneering at me. A red, puckered scar ran down his cheek. It turned white when he laughed in my face. After what seemed like an eternity, he let me go. I was free, but I stood frozen. I couldn't move. I couldn't breathe. My heart pounded as I looked into his bloodshot eyes. 'Aren't ye going to save yer friend?' he said and pulled back his fist to hit me. My senses returned just in time to dodge the blow. I darted through his legs, then overboard after Henry. I reached him, but I wasn't strong enough pull him to the docks. I could barely keep his head afloat and nearly drowned myself for trying.

Then suddenly, my da was there and another man, and they pulled Henry and me to safety."

"Did Henry survive?" she asked.

"Aye, though he never went near water again."

She stopped, turning to face him. "Ye saved him though, keeping his head afloat while ye waited for help."

He looked down into her eyes. "After the man released me, for moments, breaths, I just stood there—tethered to nothing but my own fear. I vowed that day never to allow fear to be my guide again. If I am afraid, that is when I act the fastest. When fear strikes me, I hear that man's laughter in my head. I smell his breath." Rory shrugged. "Some have called me reckless; I say I'm breaking free."

She smiled then. "I believe I called ye a reckless knave."

"Reckless to be sure, but a knave?" He slowly shook his head, drawing closer. "I think ye'll discover that I'm gentle," he said, his soft voice like a whispered caress. "A good man." He cupped her cheek, his thumb outlining her bottom lip. She closed her eyes against the sweet ache of his touch. Clenching her fists, she dug her fingernails into her palms as she fought to regain control over her racing heart.

"Anyway," she said briskly while she moved out of reach, "yer fear saved yer life. For had ye leapt into the water sooner, yer da may not have gotten to ye in time, and both of ye would have died. Then where would that leave me?"

Smiling, he reached for her hand and pulled her back, wrapping his arm around her waist. Lightning bolts of desire shot through her. His lips were so close to hers. "Ye tell me," he rasped. "Where would ye be without me?"

She wanted to kiss him. With her every thought, every breath, with every beat of her heart, she wanted to kiss him.

But she couldn't.

She had to remember that her people came first.

"I...I wouldn't have my necklace," she stammered as she gently pushed against his chest and stepped free from his arms.

Grasping her horse's reins, she started forward. The land had begun to change, the cliffs slowly subsiding into green earth once more. Trudging carefully down the steep slope, she stopped near the water where a narrow pass hugged the coastline. It felt cooler by the sea. She inhaled the crisp air, inviting its calming effect. With her mind clear, she could focus once again on the mission ahead. Reaching into one of her saddlebags, she grabbed a fistful of oats and offered the snack to Rory's mare.

"Tether her to one of those rocks," she said, pointing to a series of protruding stones. "And ride with me. She'll only be in the way."

Rory looked unconcerned. "She's a brave horse and takes direction. Do not worry about her."

"Trust me," Alex said, lifting her tunic high and pulling herself into the saddle. Then she slid forward to allow Rory room to swing up behind her.

Rory frowned for a moment, confused about why he would have to leave his mare, but then he drank in the sight of Alex pressed against the front of her saddle, her tangled, flaxen hair, cascading down her back.

"Right," he said, sliding to the ground. "Sorry, lass," he whispered to his horse, stroking her thick mane. "Ye have to sit this one out. Ye must ken there are offers too sweet to refuse."

He turned to look up at Alex. As usual, she met his gaze dead on, never resorting to the coy affectations so often used by the fairer sex. Already his pulse began to race, and he hadn't even touched her yet. He reached up and grabbed the horn of the saddle, his fingers close to the apex of her thighs. She sucked in a sharp breath. Her eyes narrowed on him with an intensity that fueled his desire. He swung up behind her and wrapped his arms around her waist, pulling her flush against him.

"Hold on tightly," she breathed.

He nosed her hair to the side, bringing his forehead down on her shoulder. "Happily," he said softly, savoring the feel of her strong, sleek body, hot against his.

"'Tis not far," she said, her voice strained. He knew the fierce attraction that pulsed from their bodies, penetrating the other, intruded upon her every thought as it did his.

They trotted along the rocky pass, waves lapping against the ridged wall that tamed the frigid water on one side. On the other, craggy, teeming cliffs renewed their stake on the land. His fingers splayed wide against her stomach. He could have held her for all eternity. Up ahead the coastline curved, revealing the dark mouth of a cave, and he knew that all too soon he would have to relinquish his prize.

"Welcome to my secret armory," she said, reining in her horse at the foot of the cave.

Rory slid to the ground and reached up to clasp her waist. She pressed her hands against his chest while he slowly lowered her to the ground.

"Trust me," she said, the corner of her mouth lifting in a sideways smile. "Ye're about to see something ye'll want even more than a good ride."

He cocked his brow at her. "I will be the judge of that."

She turned and reached into one of her large saddlebags and withdrew a thick rope, a torch, and a chard of flint. "Follow me," she said. "And bring my horse."

The cave floor was smooth, the stone worn by rushing waves, but as they moved deeper into the stone hollow, jagged rocks emerged, untouched by salt or spray. Firelight from the torch Alex had lit danced on the ceiling, casting flickering shadows on the craggy walls. They continued forward, the tunnel worming to the right, and then the passage widened. Off to the side, Rory spied a long, narrow wagon, and beyond that the path abruptly ended.

"But where are the weapons?" he asked, turning around to scan the tunnel. He crossed to the wagon for a closer look, but it, too, was empty.

"Come closer," Alex said, sliding the torch into a waiting sconce. He crossed to her side, his eyes following her downward gaze into a black pit, which preceded the tunnel's end. Eyes wide, he looked at her, a slew of questions on his tongue. But then he noticed her hands busily tying one end of the rope around her waist.

"What are ye about?" Rory said, not liking the direction things were going.

"I'm going down there," she said simply.

"Absolutely not," he blurted, grasping her arm.

She jerked free from his hold. "Do ye honestly think I will heed yer refusal? I do what I wish, Rory MacVie. That is something ye should not soon forget." She gave him the other end of the rope to hold. "Anyway, I lack the strength for what is to come. I need yer brawn up here."

Before he could protest further, she knelt at the edge of the drop. "Ready yer stance," she said.

He gripped the rope and anchored his foot behind him, preparing to bear her weight to the bottom of the pit. He slowly lowered her down, her feet and legs first disappearing into shadow. He stared hard into her eyes, while darkness overtook her waist and then her shoulders. The instant before the black pit swallowed her unflinching eyes, he froze, battling with himself to keep from pulling her back to the surface.

"*Alba gu bràth*," she said softly.

He nodded, took a deep breath, and lowered her the rest of the way. A moment later, the tension eased from the rope.

"I can feel yer worry from down here," she said, her voice laced with amusement. "Be at ease, Rory. This is hardly the most dangerous thing I've done for the cause."

That he did not doubt.

The sound of clanging metal reached his ears the instant before she called up, "'Tis time to put yer strength to good use. Pull up the first crate."

He yanked on the rope. Whatever was attached to the other end weighed significantly more than she. He spread his legs and braced himself. Then he heaved back, crossing one hand over the other and hauled her treasure to the surface. A large crate appeared, wrapped in hide, the sides of which were joined together by a thick metal ring tied to the rope.

"Go ahead and look at what's inside," she called up.

Rory untied the rope and sent it back down to her. Then he pulled back the hide flaps. Even in the dim torchlight, metal blades gleamed. A new hunger grew inside of him when he inspected one of the swords. "*Alba gu bràth*," he whispered solemnly. Then he called down to Alex, "Wait until Abbot Matthew sees these."

There were seven crates in all. Rory could not believe his eyes as he loaded each one into the wagon. "There must be nearly two-hundred swords here."

"Two-hundred and seven to be exact," she called up.

His gaze returned, taking in the sight of Scotland's swords.

"Ahem...I require yer assistance?"

He crossed back to the pit and lowered the rope. An instant later, he started to pull her up to the surface. The moment their eyes locked, he said, "Ye ken the last time ye said those words to me I undressed ye."

She reached out for him when she was close enough. He took hold of her, lifting her the rest of the way.

"Before I left my chambers today, I promised Rosie my clothes would stay on."

He shook his head to show his disapproval. "That's very disappointing." Then he gestured to the wagon. "That being said, I wouldn't advise sewing one of those into yer tunic."

Her eyes flashed with the same excitement that was coursing through his veins. "They are magnificent, are they not?" She crossed to her horse's side and freed a large, thin oilcloth from one of her bags and spread it out over the weapons.

"Ye're magnificent," he said softly, coming up behind her.

She turned and faced him, placing her hands on his strong chest. Firelight set his black hair aflame while shadow obscured his features, making his deep-set eyes even more intense, more sinful. She seized his tunic. "How do ye do this to me?" she rasped, closing her eyes against the sight of his full lips. She cleared her throat and stepped free.

"Thank ye for coming to me," she said, her voice shaky with need as she began to hitch her horse to the wagon. "For three years, Scotland's weapons have waited at the bottom of that pit, protected by wood and hide. I never could have retrieved them on my own."

Rory stood, forcing his feet to remain planted where they were when all he wanted to do was pull her back into his arms and never let go again. Damn her title. Damn her duty to her people. His fists clenched against the hunger that held his senses captive. Never had he wanted a woman more, and yet he knew she could never be his.

He drew a deep breath before joining her near the shaft of the wagon. Wordlessly, they fitted the rein terret and adjusted the straps around her stallion, their movements hasty and rough. The beast snorted in protest.

"Whoa," Alex said, stroking a soothing hand down his mane.

Rory watched her, thinking he was no better than a wound-up horse. By the Saints, he needed to regain control. Drawing another, deeper breath, he offered her his hand and helped her up into the wagon. Then he took hold of the reins and led them from the cave.

When they emerged, the sun had begun its descent, dipping close to the horizon. The fresh air served to clear his mind, and he resolved to lighten the air.

"Now where to?" he said with forced brightness.

"To Leslie MacKenzie's," she said, meeting his gaze for the first time since their most recent near kiss. "Follow back the way we came, then head east."

After they tethered Rory's mare to the back of the wagon, they cleared the slope and started out across the moors, the myriad colors of sunset behind them. Rory asked, "And when do we make the run south to the abbot?"

She drew a thoughtful breath. "I must think of an excuse for my absence. It will be at least another week if not a fortnight before I am ready. Turn down there," she said, pointing to a croft in the distance.

"We could just keep going," he said, drawing her gaze. "Ye and I, right now. Let's not stop." His smile challenged her to accept, for he knew the sooner the mission was over the sooner they could part ways. And although he hated to leave her, he knew with every moment that passed his feelings for her grew.

She seemed to consider his plan. "Mary and Rosie would make up some excuse for me. They would likely claim that I've locked myself away in my chamber for some reason or another." But then she shook her head. "Tomorrow is Lammas. I couldn't possibly leave."

"Of course," he said. "I had forgotten. Am I to guess there is to be a celebration?"

"To be sure," she answered.

"With music?"

"To be sure."

"And dancing?"

"To be sure."

"Will ye dance with me?" By all that's holy, he couldn't resist. Mayhap he was a knave?

She hesitated.

He nudged her gently with his elbow. "Ye're supposed to answer 'to be sure.'"

She laughed just as the wagon bumped, knocking her against him, causing her to laugh all the harder. "We'll see," she said, catching her breath. Then she pointed to a wood and thatch outbuilding some distance away from a cottage. "Bring the wagon right into that storehouse."

"What sort of man is Leslie MacKenzie?" Rory asked. Hopping down, he unhitched and untethered the horses.

"Trust me," she said. "He won't mind if we leave our wagon here."

Brows drawn, Rory cautioned her. "What if he runs off with the wagon? It holds a small fortune. 'Tis enough to tempt any man."

A slight smile curved Alex's lips before she took his hand and pulled him outside toward the cottage just as an old man with a stooped back came limping outside.

"Stay silent. Don't let him know ye're here," Alex whispered to Rory before she jogged over to meet the man. "Good eventide, Leslie."

The old man turned up his weathered face, revealing large, milky white eyes. "Is that ye, my lady?"

Alex wrapped her arms around the man's frail shoulders, giving him a tight squeeze. "Aye, 'tis me."

"Bless me, but it's been an age."

"I was away for a month," she explained. "And then my da died."

"I wasn't accusing ye, lass, just counting my blessings," Leslie said, his unseeing eyes pointing heavenward. "Will ye come in for a spell? I've some hot pottage."

"Forgive me, but I cannot," she said. "I am needed at Luthmore, but I brought ye something." She reached out and pressed a small, fist-sized bundle into his palm.

"Ah," Leslie said, smiling. "Ye brought me some honeycomb."

"Indeed, I did," she said, surprised that he had guessed correctly.

He brought the parcel to his nose and inhaled deeply. "Ye've paid me a short but sweet visit to be sure."

Alex pressed a kiss to the man's cheek then turned him about. "Go back inside. Darkness is upon us."

"Day or night, makes no difference to me," the man said, chuckling. "Come back and visit me soon, won't ye? And then ye can introduce me to the man ye're trying to hide."

Alex froze. She should have known Leslie would have sensed Rory's presence, even though he hadn't made a sound.

Leslie waved his hand dismissively. "Don't go confessing the truth to me now. I'll meet him at yer wedding."

"But—" Alex started to deny that Rory would ever be her husband, but Leslie had turned and held up his hand to stop her.

"Lassie, I may be blind, but that just means I can see what others can't. There's a man standing over there," he said, pointing to the exact spot where Rory stood. "And his heart pounds for ye, and yers pounds for him. Just like mine pounds for this honeycomb."

Alex watched while he shuffled away chuckling. "Aye, lass," he called back. "Love takes many forms."

She turned to face Rory whose eyes were wide with surprise. "We really need to smother whatever this is between us," she said.

Rory slowly nodded his head as he continued to watch Leslie's departure. "Apparently so."

She turned on her heel and hastened toward her horse. A moment later, Rory was beside her, his fingers laced to help her astride.

"Nay," she said, pointing him away. "Ye just stay over there, Rory MacVie!"

She hiked up her tunic and hauled herself into place. Then without waiting for Rory, she kicked her horse hard in the flanks and raced off across the violet moors, hoping to outrun her own desire.

# Chapter Twelve

Rory walked among the long trencher tables that were lined with platters of roasted meats and loaves of bread that had been blessed that very morning. The Lammas festival stretched across the field outside the outer wall of Luthmore Castle, allowing space for feasting, games, and pipers playing lively reels to which young and old danced in merry circles. Rory scanned the grounds, not in search of amusement, but for unbound, flaxen hair. He had not spoken to Alex since she had ridden away from him the night before as if the Devil himself had licked at her heels. As he scanned the revelers, his conscience pricked. Distancing himself from Alex was the honorable thing to do. His hands closed into tight fists as he resolved to do just that, but then he spotted her. She sat on a bench at one of the crowded tables beside Robert.

Rory narrowed his eyes on the golden-haired knight. Robert was a decent man, and according to Rosie, handsome enough to forgive his loquacious tongue and apparently horrid singing voice. Rory reached for a tankard of ale while he observed the pair. Robert's tongue appeared as active as usual. Alex had not spoken a word to her dinner companion, no doubt because she had not been given the chance. What's more, despite the din of chatter, laughter, and music, she did not lean toward Robert to better hear his words. In fact, she sat back, her body not truly engaged in their conversation, while her eyes wandered, scanning the crowds. Rory watched her, hoping she searched the festivities for him.

Once more, guilt nagged at him. He had no business spying on her or delighting in her disinterest in her suitors. If anything, he should be hoping for her sake and for the sake of her people that one of the men chosen by the abbot would be found worthy.

But that was just it, he wanted to scream. None of them were good enough for her.

Not that Rory was. But at the very least he fully understood the majesty that was Alex MacKenzie.

Robert was too feckless to appreciate the varied tapestry of her character. If she chose Adam, she would have to yield to convention, or they would never see eye to eye and would be unhappy. Rory imagined her life with Sir Adam Lennox, trapped within the confines of wimple and lace, her spirit choked from her enshrouded body—beautiful and unfeeling as a statue meant only to be looked at and admired from a distance. He grew angry just thinking about it.

And then there was Timothy who was gentle and good. He would be kind to Alex and to her people, but could he ignite her soul?

Rory could—that much he knew for certain. There was something unnamable that existed between them, a connection that ran soul-deep. He had felt it shoot through him the very moment they first locked eyes that night in the woods.

He turned to look over at her, but she was gone. He scanned the crowd and found her sitting beside Timothy, surrounded by children. Clearly, Timothy was telling them all a story. As she listened, a smile stretched her lips so wide it made his heart ache. Rory stiffened. Mayhap he was mistaken and some small spark did flicker between Alex and Timothy. When

Timothy looked at her, he smiled with open admiration. But then he would appreciate her unpretentious ways, her plainly spoken truth, and the way she cared for her people. Likewise, she would be drawn to Timothy's compassion.

"God's blood, he may as well be a priest," Rory grumbled to himself, reaching for a fresh tankard to cool his growing ire. He threw his head back, downing the amber liquid. Then he reached for another. If holy was what she wanted, Rory was holy. He attended Mass...at least on occasion. And he had gone to confession...once a year at the most. And he had been known to tell children stories, albeit scary ones.

"Damnation," he cursed aloud, grabbing a full tankard from a passing serving maid's tray. He swallowed it down, then reached for another and downed that one, too.

His vision blurred. He narrowed his eyes on an approaching female form, her hips swaying back and forth. He held his breath, hoping for Alex to emerge into clarity. Instead, it was one of the lassies he had spoken to during dinner when they had first arrived at Luthmore.

"Dance with me, Rory," she purred.

He glanced at Alex who now sat in private with Timothy, her hand resting intimately on his arm.

Rory took the maid's offered hand and kissed it. "My pleasure."

BECAUSE TIMOTHY HAD begged her confidence, Alex leaned closer to him to ensure their conversation was not overheard.

"There is a matter of delicacy that I wished to discuss with ye," Timothy began. "Over these last days I've come to believe that ye and I are not so dissimilar. In fact, we complement each other rather well."

Alex tensed while she listened. Was Timothy about to propose to her? She gripped her skirt tightly as she fought to stay calm. Was this not what she had hoped for—one of the three suitors setting himself apart from the others? Surely, a proposal achieved just that, making Timothy the obvious choice. But her heart ached as if it had sprouted lungs and a mouth of its very own and now sat within her chest screaming for dear life.

"Nay," she suddenly blurted.

Timothy's brows pinched together. He drew back. "Forgive me, Lady Alexandria, I thought we had a meeting of minds, a friendship if ye will?"

She reached out and took his hand, feeling guilty for having hurt him. "We are friends," she said. "Please continue."

He eyed her skeptically for a moment, but then he relaxed and leaned closer. "I wish to join the priesthood," he whispered.

Her eyes widened in surprise. Laughter bubbled up her throat, which she choked back down with a cough. "But of course ye do," she said. Having gotten over her initial shock, she realized she wasn't surprised in the least. "Ye would find true fulfillment as a priest."

Timothy nodded. "I feel it is my calling, but my father disapproves."

"But why?" she asked. "Ye do yer family a great honor."

Timothy shook his head. "My father says that it is right and good for a third son, but as his second son, he has forbidden me."

She patted his arm comfortingly. "Ye must speak to him again. Tell him ye wish to relinquish the advantages of your birthright to yer younger brother."

A flash of coal-black hair caught her eye, and she looked over then to see Rory take Alison's hand and kiss it before pulling her into a lively reel.

Alex's clenched her fists. "Excuse me, Timothy," she said, standing.

"Of course, my lady, and I thank ye for yer counsel."

Her gaze quickly darted from Rory back to the gentle man at her side. "The abbot will be joining us here at Luthmore in a little over a fortnight. Perhaps ye should speak with him on this matter."

"I do believe the abbot has guessed where my heart lies," Timothy said.

Alex did her best not to smile. "I am confident that Abbot Matthew is very unaware of just how much ye want to be a priest. Trust me. When he visits, talk to him."

Timothy nodded. "I will," he said with resolve.

Her smile vanished the moment she turned and saw how closely Rory held Alison in his arms. She stormed across the field.

"Lady Alexandria," Adam said, stepping in front of her.

She came up short, nearly bumping into him. "Forgive me, Sir Adam, I cannot—"

He thrust a full tankard at her. Some of the contents sloshed to the ground. "I brought you an ale so that we might toast Lammas together."

She took the cup from him and raised it high before downing the warm drink.

"Join me for a dance?" Adam asked.

She looked over at Rory who laughed at something Alison had said.

She reached for Adam's drink and downed that too. Then she grabbed his hand and pulled him toward the dancers, laughing loudly at a quip he never made.

RORY STOPPED SHORT and scowled as he watched Alex and Adam join the other dancers. His scowl deepened when she threw her head back in laughter.

Unlike Robert, Adam made very reasonable conversation. He was intelligent, thoughtful, kind, and even Rory could see that he was handsome. Despite his self-importance, he was clearly not out of the running. In fact, Adam was probably in the lead. He pictured Adam and Alexandria as lord and lady of Luthmore castle.

"Enough," Rory growled.

Alison jerked away from him. "Fine," she snapped. "Ye don't have to take the ale. I was only asking if ye were thirsty."

He hadn't realized that Alison had brought him another drink until that moment.

"Thank ye," Rory said as he took the cup, his eyes ever fixed on Alex. He threw it back in one gulp, then wiped his sleeve across his mouth and stormed toward the lady who was standing far too close to Adam.

"WOULD YE LOOK AT THOSE fools?" Mary said to Michael.

Together, they had been watching Rory and Alex for some time. Rory had been dancing with Alison while his eyes remained fixed on Alex. Meanwhile, Alex danced with Adam, but she kept on laughing too loudly.

Another peal of laughter reached Michael's ears. "I like Adam. He's a fine man, and I've heard him tell an amusing jest or two. But he is certainly not that funny."

"No one is," Mary said, wincing. "She sounds like an injured bird."

Michael shook his head as both Alex and Rory each downed another tankard of ale. "Both appear to be enjoying their cups more than their dance partners."

"Oh dear," Mary said, shielding her eyes with her hands. "Rory appears to be on the move. Please, tell me he is not going to confront Adam?"

Michael leaned forward. "Rory has stumbled a little. He's teetering. He may pass out. Nay, he has found his footing and is once more on the move. He is speeding up. He's almost upon them. He's pulling back his fist." Michael winced. "And...Adam is down."

"What," Mary exclaimed, dropping her hands from her eyes. She spotted Adam on the ground clutching his face in pain. "Oh dear," she said, standing. "I will go to him."

Michael shook his head at the sight of Mary racing to Adam's side. "It would seem my little Mary is not as uninvolved in this tangled love web as she believes."

He chuckled and downed the contents of his own mug. It was Lammas after all. His disapproval could wait for the morrow.

"Saints preserve us," he said out loud as Robert suddenly entered the fray and appeared to confront Rory on Adam's behalf. But then Alex stepped between the two men. He watched Alex lay into Robert and winced, having been on the receiving end of one of her rants more times than he cared to remember. A moment later, Robert stomped off, leaving Alex and Rory alone in what appeared to be a heated debate.

With a dejected look upon his face, Robert was heading back toward the keep.

"Poor sod," Michael muttered. "Robert," he called out. "Sit and have an ale with me."

Brows drawn, Robert sat down and took a long swig from a fresh cup. "Thank ye," he said with a heavy sigh. Then he turned and faced Michael. "Lady Alexandria does not seem to be at all fond of me."

Michael could not help but feel sorry for Robert. "Forget the good lady for now and let us enjoy an ale on Lammas." Then he pressed his lips together and silently cursed his own goodness, already regretting what he was about to say. "So, I hear ye know a wee something about horses?"

Straightway, Robert's face brightened.

# Chapter Thirteen

"Have ye gone mad?" Alex railed at Rory, pointing to Adam whose head rested in Mary's lap, the hem of her tunic wadded to absorb the blood gushing from his nose.

Rory firmed his stance for battle. "We've already established that I'm mad. In fact, I believe yer very words were 'reckless knave.'" He took a step closer, not a bit sorry for having punched Adam in the face, likely breaking his perfect nose. In fact, he felt better than he had in days. And he would feel even better with Alex in his arms.

Her eyes flashed. "Ye didn't have to punch him!"

"I ken," he growled, wrapping his arm around her waist. "But I've a fire blazing within me, and I had to cool it down somehow." Then he pulled her against him. "I want to be alone," he breathed. His hand shook with restraint as he gently stroked the back of his fingers down her silky, pale cheek. Then he cupped her face. "I am going to kiss ye, Alex, long and hard. Either I do it now in front of yer clan and precious suitors, or ye lead me to where we can be alone."

She sucked in a sharp breath, pushing him away. "Ye read my letter!"

He narrowed his eyes on her. "Ye left it out in the open, then let me into yer solar, alone. Ye're not a careless woman, Alex. Whether ye knew it at the time or not, ye wanted me to see it."

"What?" she scoffed. "That makes no sense. Why would I want ye to see it?"

He crushed her against his chest. "To save ye from marrying someone ye don't love."

Her eyes bore into his with an intensity that belied her denials. Still, she shook her head while at the same time, putting her arms around his neck. "I must do what is proper," she whispered, her voice growing increasingly desperate.

"Doing what's proper is just about the worst thing a lassie like ye could do."

Her stomach flipped. She gazed into his burning sky-blue eyes and grabbed his hand, leading him toward the outer wall to the secret passage that led to her chambers. Beneath the ground it was musky and dark. She removed the scorched torch from its sconce and felt for one of the chards of flint she kept on the ground. Moments later, a fire, which mirrored her burning desire, chased away the darkness. She turned around. The fire set his black hair aglow. His eyes bored into hers. She stared at his full lips—lips that had been burned forever into her memory. He continued to stare at her. She stared back, her heart pounding. Then he grabbed her by the waist and thrust her against the wall, his lips seizing hers. She wrapped her arms around his neck and pressed herself into him. Her hands moved to cup his rough, chiseled jaw and then caressed his strong shoulders.

He groaned and stepped back, raking his hand through his hair. He stared at her swollen, parted lips. The pulse throbbed at her neck. He burned for her as he had never done before. His body ached. He fought against his pulsing need. How could he resist? There was no other woman like Alex. And the fire burning through his body was mirrored in her own hungry eyes and could be heard in her gasping breaths.

"It cannot be helped," he growled, pulling her close once more. His hands wove through her hair. Her soft, golden waves tangled around his fingers as he crushed her lips against his. She clutched his face between her hands, her tongue plunging into his, caressing, teasing, stoking his passion to new heights. With a groan, he tore his lips from hers and turned her around. With quick, desperate motions, he began to untie the laces of her surcote. The fabric gave way and dropped to the ground. Then he whisked her tunic over her head. She turned back into his arms. He stared hungrily at her full breasts, their taut peaks pressed against the thin fabric of her kirtle. He moaned as she cupped her own breasts, her breathing hard and hungry. Then she reached for the belt around his waist, tugging at his tunic at the same time.

"If ye were wearing a plaid, I would have ye naked in my arms by now," she said, straining to free his body from his layers of clothing.

He pulled her against him, smiling wickedly. "I vow to wear a plaid evermore," he said, his voice husky. He slowly leaned down and caught her bottom lip gently between his teeth. Then he kissed her slowly, his tongue sweeping her mouth in languid strokes while he unclasped his belt. He broke their kiss only to pull his tunic over his head.

Her hand splayed out against his rock-solid chest, dusted with a light sprinkling of crisp, black curls. She raked her hands down his lean torso before she grabbed his muscled shoulders and pressed her body against his. Her lips claimed his, then moved down his throat, pausing over his racing pulse. The cords in his neck flexed as she continued her slow caress, savoring the salty taste of him. She licked the soft place behind his ear, then continued down, kissing and laving the taut skin of his shoulders and across his chest. She had known sexual hunger before, but never had she experienced such need. An ache, searing and hot burned between her legs. Her heart pounded harder and harder, her breathing ragged as her hands swept down and felt the full, hard length of him.

Rory's breath hitched when her palm rubbed against his swollen member. With a growl, he grabbed her, pressing the heat of her against his hardness. He backed her against the stone wall, dropped to his knees, and lifted the hem of her kirtle. He kissed the soft skin of her thighs, parting her legs and raising her kirtle higher. He could smell her desire, rich and hot. With his mouth and tongue, he slowly coaxed her thighs open. Then he buried his lips in her soft pillow of curls and found her sensitive nub, his tongue moving in gentle circles. Slowly, he slid his finger inside her. God, she was tight...so tight.

He faltered.

She was too tight.

His body shuddered as he eased his finger from her slick warmth and rested his head against her quivering body.

"Please, don't stop," she cried, the same pain that was shooting through his body echoed in her cry.

He took a deep breath, fighting to bring his own body back under control. Then his touch returned to the heat of her, stroking her, savoring the renewed sound of her soft moans. When she cried out, her body shuddered in wave after sweet wave around his touch.

"Rory," she cried as soft pants escaped her lips. "That was...I've never..."

"Hush, lass," he crooned in her ear. "Catch yer breath."

He held her close, savoring the feel of her body in his arms. His own body still throbbed with need. He fought the desire to lay her on the ground and bring her once again to the heights of passion, but then her hands came to life. She wrapped her arms around his neck, her full lips claiming his.

"Nay," he said, setting her at arms-length. He took the torch from the sconce and gestured deeper into the cave. "Ye go that way, and I'll return the way we came."

"But Rory—"

"Nay," he said. Then he kissed her once more before taking several steps back. "Ye've saved yer maidenhead for yer husband." He took another step back. "It will be yer husband who takes it. Go now."

She hesitated another moment before she turned and hastened toward the keep. He watched her until she dipped from sight around the bend.

"And yer husband will be me," he whispered aloud.

# Chapter Fourteen

The next morning, Alex walked onto the high dais and softly gasped. Rory stood in the rear of the great hall clad as promised in naught but the MacKenzie plaid. She drank in the sight of his muscular arms and his broad, bare chest, which only hours before she had touched, tasted. Warmth flooded her core. She wet her lips, remembering the force of his kiss, his hot breath on her neck, and the agonizing pleasure of his touch. He smiled slowly, sensually. Overcome with desire, she lifted the hem of her tunic and dashed down the stairs, but the creaking hinges of the great door shortened her flight. Heart pounding, she masked her hunger behind a welcoming smile.

"Good morrow," she said to Michael and her three unknowing suitors.

A bruise framed the bridge of Adam's nose and darkened the skin around his eyes. He did not return her greeting. Instead, he glared at Rory. Robert, on the other hand, dipped his head in a respectful bow, but his smile did not reach his eyes. Michael also appeared tense. Timothy alone received her with genuine goodwill. Unfortunately, Timothy wanted to be a priest. She expelled a long breath. Her pursuit of a husband was not going well.

Rory crossed to her side then, his close proximity instantly stealing her breath.

"What are ye doing?" she whispered.

He offered her his arm. "Taking ye to church."

Her heart started to pound. Only Rory could say that in a way that made it sound like a sin.

"Sir Adam will escort Lady Alexandria to Mass," Michael announced, putting emphasis on Adam's title. "Rory, I need ye in another capacity."

Alex bristled, scowling at Michael. For a moment, she hoped Rory might deny her steward, but in the end, he dipped his head in acquiescence and turned to follow Michael from the hall.

"Rory," she called out to him before realizing she had yet to invent an excuse to do so. She searched her mind, feeling the weight of everyone's eyes on her.

"This is what ye're looking for." He reached into his new sporran and withdrew her broken chain. "I fixed it for ye."

Her hand flew to her throat and felt her talisman beside his silver cross. "Thank ye," she said, taking her old chain from his hand. "That is very good of ye."

He started to turn. She grabbed his arm. "I hope to see ye after Mass."

His sky-blue eyes alone spoke his promise before he dipped his head, his lips curved in a soft smile.

She tore her eyes away, dreading the awkwardness of her waiting company, but to her immense relief, Mary suddenly appeared from behind the screen.

"Cousin," Alex exclaimed as she crossed the hall and took Mary's arm. Then, instead of rejoining the noblemen, she hastened toward the doors to the courtyard, calling out for the men to follow, thereby avoiding an offer of escort to the chapel. Although more than likely such an offer would not have been forthcoming. Both Adam and Robert were still clearly upset with her—not that she blamed them. Her conduct at the festival had been outlandish at best. But the sight of Alison in Rory's arms had driven her mad with jealously. Doubtless, her behavior had not escaped Michael's notice, which would explain his dismissal of Rory. Still, she was lady of Luthmore. How dare Michael admonish her in public? Worst yet, how could he send Rory away against her obvious wishes?

During Mass, she struggled to block out Robert's strangled crooning all the while her tongue sharpened and her agitation with Michael grew.

After everyone had filed out into the courtyard, she charged at Michael who sat in wait with the stable master. "We must speak."

Michael nodded curtly and led Alex out of the courtyard. Together, they circled the outer wall. When they reached the far side, she laid into him.

"Where is Rory?"

"I put him to work in the fields as is his station."

"Ye sent him to labor in the fields? What is the matter with ye? He is our guest!"

Michael's eyes flashed. "What of yer duty? Is that not the more pressing question?"

Fury pulsed through her. She snatched the veil from her head, then turned her back on him. "My laces if ye please," she snapped.

"Alex—" Michael began.

"My laces if ye please!"

She felt Michael fumble with the laces of her fine surcote. Finally, it loosened and fell about her waist. She pushed it down and stepped free from the thick embroidered fabric.

Then she picked it up and tossed it at him before storming away.

"Where are ye going?"

"To make the rounds," she shouted back over her shoulders.

"And to venture to the fields, no doubt."

She whirled around. "What is it to ye?"

Michael closed the distance between them. "I like Rory too. There is much to admire in his character, but ye can't marry him."

Alex crossed her arms over her chest. "I have said nothing of the kind."

"Ye didn't have to say it. Yer eyes have done all the talking for ye. For pity's sake, Alex, think of the people. Yer heart cannot be yer guide. The MacLeod will never forgive the insult if ye were to choose a peasant over him. Ye know this. 'Tis why ye wrote to Abbot Matthew in the first place, instead of choosing a husband from one of our own warriors."

She stiffened. Michael was right, and no amount of wishing on her part could change that. A weight settled over her, pressing down on her heart until she could hardly draw breath. Rory made her knees weak, her heart pound. He made her happy. Still, she had no business falling for him. Marrying for love was not a privilege enjoyed by noblewomen. A prudent marriage would strengthen their borders. She gripped her mother's trinity knot and remembered. The wellbeing of the people comes first, always. She had no words. An ache like a steel cage enclosed her heart. Numbly, she walked away.

The noontide sun shone down, though she did not feel its warmth. She felt cold and empty, as if her heart was being hollowed out. Childish laughter drew her eyes from the bracken-covered earth. She looked up to see a blur of limbs and big smiles racing off toward the woods, wee ones with only a year or two left to enjoy the freedom of childhood before they would take up their place within the clan, planting seed, cooking, and harvesting. She crossed a small wooden bridge that cast its shadow over a swiftly moving stream just before the road came to a fork. Right would lead her to the fields and Rory. Left meandered down to the village where her people awaited her care. Her heart thudded in her ears, not the racing heart of desire. It was the drum of doom. With a sigh, she chose left and hurried to Helen's cottage, bursting in without first knocking.

Helen's eyes widened for a moment. "Alex, are ye alright?"

Alex closed the door gently behind her. "Sorry, Helen. I...I..." She sighed. "I just missed ye."

Helen pressed her hand to her chest. "Ye sweep in here like a banshee crossing the moors. My heart's still pounding." Then she motioned to the small table in the center of the room. "Sit, love, and I'll pour ye some ale."

Alex scooped Cassie up in her arms on the way and sat down, cuddling the wee lass.

"Yer heart is heavy," Helen said.

Alex shook her head. "Nay, all is well—"

But Helen was quick to interrupt. "Don't ye try that with me. Mayhap ye can fool the rest of the world, but not me. Now, out with it. What's on yer mind?"

Tears stung Alex's eyes. She couldn't tell Helen the truth, not without revealing her secret life. "'Tis just that I saw some children racing into the woods only minutes ago. They were laughing and playing. It made me think of those days. Do ye remember?"

Helen chuckled. "Of course I do. We used to wander down to the river and pick berries until our bellies were full."

Alex swiped her wet cheeks and smiled. "Our hands would be purple for days."

Helen reached across the table and squeezed her hand. "Do ye remember that time Jean sent us picking so she could make tarts, but we ate all we could find?"

Laughter bubbled up Alex's throat. "Our faces and hands told the truth even if our tongues tried to lie."

"She didn't stay mad at us for long," Helen remembered, smiling. "She sliced us each a big piece of bread, smeared butter on it, and said she didn't blame us one bit. That she had a sweet spot for berries too."

Alex sighed. "Those were good days."

"Aye, they certainly were, but why are ye visiting the old days? What's happened?"

Alex quickly scanned Helen's sparsely furnished cottage. How could she complain about her lot in life to Helen? Helen awoke before dawn and started her fire. She made Gregor breakfast before he left to work the fields. She had five children all under the age of nine. She cooked, cleaned, and toiled from before sun-up until after dark—and she had no choice, while Alex chose to labor. She chose to make her life a service to her people. The only advantage afforded Helen's station was that she had been lucky enough to marry for love. She had chosen Gregor while Alex certainly would never choose to marry Adam, Robert, or Timothy. Then she again remembered that Timothy longed for the priesthood, striking him from her list of suitors, which left only Robert and Adam who were both vexed with her. She cursed under her breath. Her behavior the day before had complicated an already complex situation. Mayhap she didn't even have the luxury of a choice anymore. What if neither man would take her?

Alex rubbed her eyes, then sat back in her chair. "I do not ken what's wrong with me. I suppose seeing those children just made me long for those carefree days." She finished her cup and stood up. "Anyway," she said with forced brightness, "I will carry on with rounds and let ye get back to cooking."

Helen frowned. "Ye look tired. Finish yer rounds and then go take a rest."

"I will if ye will," Alex said with a wink, knowing Helen would have to be near death to sleep in the middle of the day.

She stepped back outside and lifted her face to the sky. The sun shone bright and warm and directly overhead. She chewed her lip, debating whether to return to Luthmore for the noon meal. She turned her back on the castle. Too many men awaited her there, and at that moment, there was only one man she wished to see.

"I miss ye, Da," she muttered under her breath.

With so many villagers up at the keep, the naked paths beckoned her with their openness, their quiet. They promised clarity. She would have no place to hide, even from herself. She wandered the roads, imagining her father still walked at her side. As if in a dream, cottages floated past like gray, shifting clouds while her mind focused on her father's imaginary counsel. Gently, he placed Michael's truth deep inside her heart, his voice as soft as a feather sashaying through air. Her life was not her own; it belonged to her people.

"Does anyone's life belong to themselves alone?" she whispered aloud.

*Only those with no one to share it with.*

The truth was weightless in its simplicity.

Feeling resolute, she scanned her surroundings with renewed focus. She had unknowingly wandered beyond the village outskirts. Her eyes traced the distant castle. Then shifting her feet, she drank in the sight of rugged mountains set far against the heavens. Again, she turned, but her newly claimed calm fled her soul as she gasped and stumbled forward, her eyes wide with disbelief. Thick ribbons of smoke coiled up from the roof of a distant crofter's storehouse. An instant later, she was running. Cries for help reached her ears, and she pushed her body harder, racing against the hungry flames.

Two feminine figures came into view. Margaret, the crofter's wife, and her daughter, Anna, hoisted buckets of water at the blaze. Ash and smoke blackened their faces and tunics. Despite their desperate struggle, the fire yielded nothing. Alex rushed past them without stopping and dashed inside, wanting to save as many bags of seed as she could. What if disease swept through the village, or one of their neighbors attacked? They could not afford a smaller harvest. The risks were too great.

"Nay, my lady, ye mustn't," she heard Margaret scream.

Alex barreled out through the door, stooped over from the weight of the heavy sack on her shoulder. "Send for help!"

"Go, Anna! Go to the keep," Margaret cried.

Thick smoke choked the air. Alex covered her mouth with her arm as she burrowed once again into the burning store. She reached for another bag of seed, but then above the din of splintering wood and thatch and the roaring fire, she heard the bleating of panicked sheep. Straining beneath the weight of the seed bag, she bent over and hastened toward the door and dumped it off her back when she reached the pile she had made safely beyond the destructive lick of the flames.

Then Alex turned around. The fire had spread now across the roof and up one side. Still, the bleating sounded from within. Without hesitation, she rushed back inside.

RORY PUMPED HIS ARMS, running as fast as he could toward the black smoke curling toward the sky. He could hear a woman screaming for help and the breaths of the men running just behind him. By the time they reached the long storage hut, the roof was engulfed in flames.

"She ran inside," the woman screamed, racing at him.

"Who ran inside?" Rory said, grabbing her shoulders.

"Alex," she cried. "She's going to save them."

"Alex," he shouted, pushing past her. He pulled the plaid from his body and plunged it in the nearby trough. Then hanging the fabric over his head, he barreled through the blackened doorway. Blazing heat scorched his skin.

"Alex," he shouted. "Alex!"

"Rory," she cried. "I'm here."

His eyes stung as he tried to see through the smoke. He rushed in the direction of her voice, but then a creak rent the air. He looked up just as part of the ceiling gave way. He dove to escape the fiery embers.

"Alex!"

"I'm surrounded by fire!"

Through licking flames and billowing smoke, he saw the shift of her silhouette. Her racking cough reached his ears. He pulled the plaid low over his head and leapt through the flames. She stood, hunched over in the corner, coughing and huddling around a cluster of sheep.

"Where are the others?" he shouted above the roar of the flames.

"What others?" she croaked.

"The ones ye're saving."

"Here," she said, gesturing to the sheep.

"For the love of God, Alex!" He cried. Then he threw the wet plaid over her. Heat blasted his bare flesh. He kicked against the thatch and log siding again and again until at last he made a large enough hole.

She started to shoo the sheep through the opening.

"Are ye mad?" he cried. "Leave them!"

But she ignored him and scurried through the hole only after the last animal had escaped. Then he crawled through on hands and knees. He lay on his back, sputtering and coughing. An instant later, the storehouse groaned as the rest of the ceiling collapsed.

ALEX COUGHED INTO HER pillow. Her throat stung. She turned to lay on her back and stared up at the ceiling. "Ye cannot force me to lie in bed for the remainder of the evening."

Mary did not look up from her embroidery. "Ye fell unconscious after having to be nearly dragged from a burning building. Yer throat is clearly raw. Ye're staying put."

"I had to save the sheep."

A knock sounded at the door. Alex prayed it was her turn to be rescued. "Come in."

Rory flung the door wide and stalked in, planting his feet wide at the foot of her bed. "Are ye telling me that ye raced into a fiery death trap only to save some sheep?"

She sat up. "Nay," she said, crossing her arms over her chest.

"Really? Then please tell me what else ye risked yer life for?"

"Sacks of grain and seed," she replied.

His scowl deepened. "Ye accuse me of being reckless when ye're madder than any agent I've ever met. How could ye put yer life on the line like that?"

She swung her blankets back and jumped out of bed, storming at him. "I am acting laird of this clan. The lives of my people are my responsibility and mine—" Her words were smothered by her cough.

He threw his hands up. "But that is the point I am trying to get into that hot head of yers. The only life at risk today was yer own. Grain and seed can be replaced. A brood of sheep can be replaced. Alex MacKenzie can never be replaced. No one's life was at stake other than yers and mine by default."

"No one's life was at risk today because of that fire. But what of tomorrow or next month or next year? What of the lambs those sheep will birth in the spring? What of the crops lost today because of the seed I couldn't save? Someone will go with less food tomorrow because of what happened today. Stores represent hope against disaster, which in the end is inevitable. That is the power of one bag of grain or one sheep. Never take anything for granted, Rory MacVie. My actions today were not to save a necklace. I did it to save my people."

Rory raked his hand through his hair while he wrestled contrasting desires. He wanted to ring her neck, but he also wanted to raise her high, higher than the stars for how well she loved her people. Inside her slim frame, she held greatness, but also blind recklessness—not that he was any better. Still, he had expected her to have more sense than him.

"Truth be known," Mary said from her seat near the hearth. "I think ye're both mad."

# Chapter Fifteen

R ory sat on a stack of grain bags and leaned back against the cool inner wall. Overhead, a canopy made from oilcloth kept the rising sun off his brow. He took a deep breath and tried to release the anxiety he'd been lugging around since he first heard that Alex had rushed into a burning building. He still could not believe what she had done. He furrowed his brow, imagining how she might respond to his judgment of her. She would accuse him of being a hypocrite, which would, of course, be true. He often acted heedless of danger, but that was different. His life mattered little when measured against the exquisiteness that was Alex MacKenzie. The mere thought of the world being denied her courage and grace was too great a sorrow for him to bear.

She had become essential to him.

He closed his eyes. At least for the moment, he didn't have to worry about her safety. She had agreed to remain in bed for one more day. He chuckled to himself. That was wholly inaccurate. Alex had certainly not agreed to remain isolated in her chamber. Mary, proving herself to be quietly resolute, and Rosie had united, making a stubborn and impassable front. Truth be told, he thought Alex had appeared well enough to move about, but he wasn't about to stand in Mary and Rosie's way. They clearly wanted to hold Alex responsible for her misguided heroics.

The drum of hooves captured his attention. He leaned forward, peering out from beneath the canopy at a rider galloping into the courtyard with Gavin at his side. A nagging apprehension filled him when he recognized Benny, the abbot's youngest agent. He hoped the lad did not bring ill tidings. Quickly sliding to his feet, he hastened toward the visitor.

"Whoa," Rory said, grabbing the horse's bit and helping Benny bring his mount to a halt.

"Nice plaid," Benny said, eying Rory's new attire.

"'Tis rather comfortable. Ye should try for yerself."

Benny laughed. "And show the lassies my scrawny legs? Absolutely not."

Gavin brought his horse alongside Rory. "He said he was a friend of yers, which is clearly true."

Rory nodded. "Indeed he is. Benny, this here is Gavin MacKenzie, captain of the guard. Gavin, meet Benedict MacTavish, one of the abbot's messengers."

Gavin nodded at Benny in greeting before turning back to Rory. "I'll leave ye both to yer business and let Finlay and Michael know of his coming." Then he turned his horse and left the courtyard through the gate.

Benny slid to the ground.

"What word from Abbot Matthew?" Rory said, his voice low.

"I wasn't sent here by the abbot. My message is from David."

"What word then from David?"

"He bids ye make haste to the Iron Shoe Tavern. He needs ye for a mission."

"Did he give ye any details?"

"He told me nothing other than he will meet you in the tavern two evenings from today."

Rory could not imagine what would be important enough to pull him away from his current mission.

"Does the abbot know?"

Benny shrugged. "He knows about David's mission. I do not ken whether he knows David sent for ye."

Rory groaned and looked heavenward. "Ye ken ye've complicated what is already a rather complex mission here."

Benny smiled. "Remember—I'm only the messenger."

Rory raked his hand through his hair. "Aye, well come on messenger. I'll take ye to the stables. Ye can wipe yer horse down and give her some fresh oats."

They stepped into the stables, and straightaway Rory spied Robert who was on his knees inspecting a newborn foal with Fergus, the stable master.

"Good morrow," Rory said, keeping a cautious eye on Robert while leading Benny's horse into an empty stall. Robert looked up. His gaze held none of the previous day's hostility. In fact, Robert smiled and looked like he was about to speak to Rory when a lassie with chestnut curls and bright, blue eyes opened the stable doors.

"Da," she called, drawing everyone's gaze.

"Aye, Cara," Fergus said, looking up.

Cara's gaze shifted from her father and locked with Rory's. She stared at him with open admiration. "Yer lunch is ready, Da." Cara said, not looking away from Rory.

"Thanks, love. Tell yer mother I'll be home after I'm done here. Robert is helping me with the new foal."

Cara smiled at Rory, a lovely rose blush tinting her cheeks, before she dipped in a curtsy and turned on her heel, disappearing the way she'd come.

Benny slowly shook his head. "Ye never cease to amaze me. No matter where ye go, the lassies turn three shades of pink at the sight of ye."

Rory shrugged, his attention still on Robert who had stood and was crossing the stables, heading toward them.

"I'm sorry for confronting ye at Lammas," Robert said, offering his hand to Rory. "Spirits ran high. Ale flowed freely. Ye ken how it is."

Rory clasped Robert's offered hand. "'Tis I who should apologize. And ye're right about the ale. I was soused. I had no right to hit Adam."

"Mary told me just this morning that Adam bears ye no ill will and neither do I." Then Robert chuckled. "It was a lively night, to be sure. My head pounded the next morning. It felt like an army marching to war across my forehead." Suddenly, Robert's easy expression vanished. Brows drawn, he said, "Have ye any word on how Alex is doing? I tried to visit her earlier, but Mary and Rosie refused me. I dread to think of what could have befallen our dear lady had ye not rescued her in time." Robert pulled a folded piece of parchment from his satchel. "I've written a poem celebrating her great heroics. Those sheep are indebted to her."

All thoughts of goodwill for Robert fled Rory's mind. "She's not accepting visitors," he snapped before storming out the stable doors.

His fists clenched. David had very bad timing. How could he leave Alex to the attentions of her poetry-wielding suitors?

The answer was simple—he couldn't. Not now, not ever.

Then he remembered their secret armory—Scotland's swords. He would just have to convince Alex to make the journey to Haddington Abbey sooner, and then whatever mission David had planned, she could take part in—after all, she was one of Scotland's agents. A slight smile curved his lips while he relished the idea of the journey south with Alex—alone. At that moment, he did not know how they would explain her departure to Michael, but he was confident they would find a way.

He turned to Benny. "Take yerself to the keep and have something to eat. Then ride back to David. Ye can take my mare. Tell him that I'll be there."

WITH PLANS HATCHING in his mind, Rory hastened to Alex's chamber. He knocked on the door.

"Who is it?" Rosie called from the other side.

"'Tis Rory."

She flung the door wide, reached out and grabbed him by the arm and yanked him inside before shutting and locking the door behind him. "I'm warning ye," she whispered. "She's in a mood, to be sure."

Rory crossed to Alex's bedside. Pale blond hair pooled behind her head.

She sat up. "Thank God ye've come," she said, her speech rushed. "Ye have to convince Mary and Rosie that I'm well enough to leave. They won't even let me out of bed."

Rory raised his brows. "Why don't ye just leave?" he said, feigning ignorance. "Surely, they do not keep ye prisoner."

"They've threatened to tell Michael that I'm one of Scotland's agents." Her eyes flashed angrily at Rosie before she turned back to look at Rory. "I'm surprised she let ye in. I haven't even seen Michael today—which means they are turning away my visitors. How did ye get past?"

"Just lucky, I suppose," he said. Then his attention was caught by Rosie who stood where Alex could not see her. Silently, Rosie acted as if she were coughing, then pointed to Alex. He bit the side of his cheek to keep from smiling. "Ah...I understand Rosie is very concerned about yer cough."

Alex threw her hands up. "What cough?" she snapped. "I've barely coughed all morning. They are punishing me for saving the sheep yesterday."

"It was a foolhardy thing to do," Rosie said, marching into view.

Alex's face turned red. "Rory, tell her that rushing into my burning stores is hardly the most reckless thing I've ever done. Ye of all men know that. Anyway," she said, crossing her arms over her chest. "I will do whatever I deem is required of me, for my people and for Scotland."

He froze, taking in her form, tucked neatly in bed. Then his gaze shifted to her nightstand where her breakfast sat untouched. He smiled. They had their perfect cover. The only two people who knew Alex was an agent were the same two people keeping her locked away in her room. No one else had gained entry today, which meant no one else knew her true condition.

He reached for her hands. "Little do Mary and Rosie know, they have just done me and Scotland a mighty favor."

"What are ye talking about?" she said, allowing him to help her to her feet.

"Join me by the hearth, and I'll tell ye."

"Ahem," Rosie said, looking pointedly at Rory. "She is supposed to stay in bed."

He flashed her a smile. "Don't fash yerself, Rosie. 'Tis just a wee mission. Well, actually two wee missions, but when we're done, I promise ye, she'll stay in bed for a week if ye want."

Rosie looked at Rory, then at Alex, then back at Rory. Finally, she threw her hands up and crossed the room, taking up some mending. "It's not as if Mary and I could stop ye both anyway."

Rory smiled and sat down, meeting Alex's eager gaze. "I've just received a message from David."

"Who's David?"

"The other agent in the woods the night we first met."

"He's talking about the man who stood by and watched him undress ye," Rosie scolded from across the room.

Rory pressed his lips together to keep from chuckling. "The same," he said. Then he turned back to Alex. "We're to meet him at the Iron Shoe Tavern in two days' time. He will give us the details then."

"He asked for my aid?"

"Nay, not exactly. Still, would ye rather stay here, imprisoned in yer own chamber?"

Alex shot Rosie an accusatory look. "Ye're right," she said, turning back to Rory. "I'll do it; that is, if we can think of an excuse for my absence. I may be Lady of Luthmore, but I am still a woman, Rory. I'm not free to come and go as I please."

"That's just it. We do not have to invent an excuse. Ye won't be leaving Luthmore at all."

"I don't understand."

"Mary and Rosie will continue to guard yer door. To all the world, ye will be ill in bed when in truth we shall be moving the weapons and helping David."

She jumped to her feet, a smile spreading widely on her lips. "That could work. My condition would have to worsen before it improved, of course. Mayhap, I could develop some kind of pox."

Rory shook his head. "A pox is too severe. A good fever will do."

Alex smiled. "I suppose ye're right. It'll have to be a fever and the chills."

"Aye," Rory agreed. "Ye'll have the chills and ragged breathing too." Then he turned to Rosie. "Are ye paying attention, Rosie? This is important."

"By the Saints, ye're both mad," Rosie said, raising her eyes heavenward.

Alex winked at Rory. "Don't worry. Rosie may protest, but secretly she delights in being a Scottish rebel. We'll just have to win Mary's support."

Just then a key turned in the door and Mary walked in.

Alex and Rory smiled at each other. Then Alex stood and greeted her cousin. "Mary, we were just talking about ye. Come and sit with me. I've a wee favor to ask."

# Chapter Sixteen

Alex stood gazing out her casement at the round moon glowing high in the star-studded sky. Anticipation shot through her.

"'Tis time," Rory said, coming to stand at her side. "I have given Michael and the others my excuses. As far as the inhabitants of Luthmore are concerned, I have journeyed south to assist the abbot."

Alex turned, her eyes traveling the length of Rory's tall, muscular form. He had traded his plaid for a faded, brown tunic and frayed brown hose.

She smiled her approval. "Ye look like the humblest of peasants."

"'Tis because I am a humble peasant. Remember?"

"A peasant ye may be, Rory MacVie, but humble?" She looked up at him and tilted her head to the side, pretending to consider the possibility. He smiled under her scrutiny, and once again she was struck by how painfully good-looking he was. She laughed. "Ye've not been humble a day in yer life." Then she fanned out her usual threadbare tunic and spun around. "How do I look."

He smiled. "Ravishing as always. Although I do believe there is something different about ye."

She lifted the hem of her skirt. "Right ye are. I'm wearing shoes."

He stepped toward her. A shiver shot up her spine when his hand, warm and strong, came to rest at her waist. "We are ready then," he said, his voice low.

She nodded, looking up into his sky-blue eyes, which glinted with excitement, mirroring her own thrill over what was to come. Whatever David's mission involved, she knew it had to be important. She knew it would bring Scotland that much closer to freedom.

Alex turned to Mary. "Be careful while I'm gone. See to the needs of our people, but, also, do not neglect yerself. In the evening, seek quiet and solitude in the chapel and give up the day's worries to God."

Mary smiled, tears flooding her golden-brown eyes. "I promise," she said and threw her arms around Alex's neck. "Ye know I hate when ye go away. Is there nothing I can say that will make ye stay put for once? Scotland has enough agents; whereas Luthmore cannot afford to lose another leader."

Alex held Mary close. "Luthmore will only remain strong if Scotland does. Anyway, Luthmore has ye, Mary, and I leave our people in yer care with full confidence." Then she pulled away just enough to wipe at Mary's tears. "Ye ken I love ye, but I must go. 'Tis my calling."

Mary nodded and drew a deep, bolstering breath. "I ken."

Alex kissed her cheek. "I will miss ye, but I shall not be away long. Mind that William stays out of trouble."

"I will," Mary said. Then she stepped away, allowing Rosie room to throw her arms around Alex.

"Mind ye don't do anything foolish," Rosie admonished.

Mary scoffed. "Given she's about to steal away into the night, smuggling weapons through lands infested with thieves, the real sort, with a gorgeous Scottish rebel. I think it's too late for that warning."

Rosie bristled, shooting a scowl at Mary. "She knows what I mean." Then Rosie turned back to look at Alex, cupping her cheeks. "Don't be foolish. No running headlong into burning buildings."

Alex pressed a kiss to Rosie's cheek. "I promise, no more great heroics."

"Och, lass, don't ye be making promises to me that ye can't begin to keep. God gave ye to Scotland so that ye could save it."

Alex smiled. "I'll do my best."

Rosie squeezed her tightly. "Now that's one promise I know ye'll keep. I love ye, lass. Yer mother'd be proud."

Alex smiled at her womenfolk, their faces blurred by a curtain of tears. Then she turned to Rory. "Are ye ready?" she asked.

Rory stepped toward Mary and dipped his head. "We should be gone less than a fortnight." Then he turned to Rosie and pressed a kiss to her plump cheek. "Keep that door shut and locked by command of yer lady. Be ready to invent illnesses as needed." Then he turned and lifted the trap door in the floor and took the offered torch from Rosie's hand. The staircase wound down, then leveled off and wormed through the ground. When they arrived at the door that would lead them beyond the outer wall, Rory stopped and looked at Alex, his eyes gleaming with longing in the torch fire. "I never would have believed so dark and dank a place could ever conjure such powerful memories."

Alex let Rory's sensual tone wash over her. She glanced at the hard, stone wall she had leaned against while his hands had boldly stroked her hardened nipples, and his touch had driven her to new heights of...

"Nay!" she blurted. "Keep walking. We must at least make it beyond the castle grounds fully clothed—or else we are just a mockery of the cause."

Under the cover of hooded cloaks and the dark of night, they set out through the forest where Rory had already prepared their wagon, covering the weapons with bags of seed.

She peeked beneath one of the bags. "At long last, these swords will make it into the hands of Scottish soldiers."

"We will meet David at the Iron Shoe. Someone there will be able to take the wagon the rest of the way to Haddington Abbey."

"He had best be trustworthy."

"Mayhap it will be a she."

She smiled. "Mayhap ye're right. The abbot is always full of surprises."

She leaned back in the wagon and watched the stars shining beyond the canopy of leaves. "I love Luthmore, but when I leave home I...I do not ken. It is hard to describe how I feel. 'Tis like a need I didn't even know I had is being satiated."

"I believe I ken what ye mean. Well, in a way. Ye see, I was always content staying home in Berwick when it was still our great city. I had no wish to leave my family or friends. Had the city not crumbled beneath the might of King Edward's hammer, I would still be happily laboring on the docks. But my elder brothers, Jack and Quinn had been fisherman once upon a time. They both loved home and hearth, but the sea called to them. The call was so mighty in Quinn's heart, he even sailed on a merchant ship for several years. That is what resides in ye.

Ye love yer family and ye honor yer duty, but ye're restless. Ye crave adventure and the unknown."

"Michael would say I'm imprudent."

"Aye, and so am I, which is why we're a perfect match."

We are a perfect match, her heart screamed. We were meant to be together.

She sat up. "Duty would argue otherwise," she whispered.

"Tonight, ye're a rebel. And our first duty is not to home and hearth and not to each other—it's to Scotland."

She grabbed the reins from his hands and gave the horses a nudge forward. "Right ye are. *Alba gu bràth!*"

They rode on for several hours, keeping constant watch on the roadside for thieves hidden among the trees. Sunrise teased the horizon, making the sky blush a soft pink. Soon, they would be able to stop and rest their horses, for daylight would banish tinkers and highwaymen deeper into the forest.

Alex sat straighter and looked at Rory. "What was that?"

He shook his head. "I don't know. It sounded like a bird being strangled."

"Mayhap, Robert followed us and is serenading the trees," Alex said, unable to resist the jest.

Rory snapped the reins, urging their tired mounts into a trot. "Ye're right," he said.

Alex raised her brows in surprise. "Rory, I promise ye, Robert is nowhere near us."

"Robert isn't, but someone else is."

Another discordant caw rent the early morning air. Alex stiffened. She scanned the forest for movement, but all was still. She reached beneath her seat and discreetly grabbed her crossbow. Holding the stirrup securely with her feet, she used both hands to pull the string back and locked it in place. Then she laid a bolt in the groove just as another call sounded from the opposite side of the road. "Hoo."

She laughed out loud. "I've never heard a worse attempt at a bird call."

Rory smiled but kept his eyes trained on the trees. "I'm fairly certain we are about to meet some—" he pulled back on his reins just as a man swung down from the trees and dropped to the ground in front of them, landing on his arse. "Robbers," Rory finished, bringing their wagon to a stop.

The man scrambled to his feet, reclaiming his club that had fallen several feet away.

"Halt," the man said when he turned to face their wagon.

Alex glanced at Rory. Then she looked back to the man. "We already have."

He scratched his matted hair. "Oh, right," he said, coming toward them. His threadbare tunic and hose hung from his rail-thin body. He pointed his club at them. "Stay where ye are." Then he turned and shouted into the woods. "Come on, Rabbit."

A moment later, a stout man with a bald head and bushy beard jumped from the bushes. He glowered at Rory and Alex, thrusting a sickle in their direction.

"What took ye so long?" the first man snapped.

"Ye didn't give me the signal, Badger, and I told ye not to call me Rabbit. Me thievin' name is Silver Hawk."

Badger rolled his eyes. "All right, Silver Hawk. Now, go check the wagon."

"'Tis only seed," Rory said.

The stout man sneered at Rory. "I'll be the judge of that."

Rory tensed as he watched the man circle around the wagon. Raising his sickle high, Silver Hawk slashed open one of the bags.

"Badger, he's right," the thief said, coming back around. But Badger didn't answer. He stared at Alex. Rory flexed his hand. His sword lay on the seat right behind him. If he needed to, he could slay both fiends before they drew their next breath. He just hoped it didn't come to that.

"We are but humble farmers. We have nothing that would interest ye," Rory said.

Badger narrowed his eyes on Alex. He spat on the ground. "I'll take that bit of silver she's wearin' around her pretty neck."

Alex smiled. "Come closer, and I'll give it to ye."

"I wouldn't do that, Badger," Rory warned.

Badger opened his mouth full of rotted teeth and laughed as he walked up to Alex. "What are ye goin' to do, farmer. Run me through?"

"Nay," Rory said. "But she might."

Alex smiled sweetly at Badger the instant before she let her cloak fall away and revealed her crossbow aimed just below his waist. "Don't move."

Rory winced. "Or at least yer bollocks."

"Tell the rest of yer men to come out," Alex said.

Eyes wide, Badger's hand moved to cup her target. "'Tis just Rabbit and me," he squeaked.

"Me name is Silver Hawk," the other man snapped.

"Shut up," Badger howled. "She's goin' to shoot an arrow into me coin purse."

Alex pressed the bow closer.

Badger squealed. "Come out, lads. Come on out."

Two more men, just as raggedy, tramped out of the woods. Alex shifted the crossbow away from Badger and pointed it at the newcomers. "All of ye, go stand over there," she said, pointing to one side of the road. They all lined up, protectively cupping their favored appendage.

"Now drop yer hose."

At her command, all five men pushed their hose down until the fabric gathered at their ankles. Then they stood straight, their eyes wide with fear.

She smiled. "Now, we will bid ye goodbye."

"I did warn ye," Rory said to Badger. Then he reached into his satchel and took out a handful of coin, which he threw at their feet. "If ye try this again, ye might lose more than yer dignity. Take that coin and find some honest work. Ye're the worst thieves I've ever seen."

RAMSAY'S BLOND HAIR shone gold in the soft candlelight. Alex watched as he ran a smooth wet stone over the blade of a sword, eying the thin edge. "Good evening Rory, Alex," he said without looking up at their approach.

Alex smiled and bent at the waist, pressing a kiss to Ramsay's cheek. "'Tis a pleasure, as always."

"How are ye, Ramsay?" Rory asked.

He rested the sword on his knee and looked up then. "I'm enjoying a beautiful summer's eve," Ramsay replied. Then he jerked his head toward the door. "David's been waiting on ye."

Alex smiled at Rory. "We were briefly detained." Then she looked around. "Has it been quiet?"

"Aye. The village sleeps. Go on ahead. Ye know I'll keep watch."

"As always, ye have our thanks," Rory said.

Alex dipped her head to the handsome blacksmith, then she turned and led the way inside. She rounded the woodpile and lifted the boards away. "After ye," she said to Rory.

He smiled. "Nay, lass. Ye go ahead."

"Suit yerself," she replied, before she dropped down through the hole. Hunched over, she crossed to the blue curtain and swept it aside.

"Hello, again," she said.

A flash of surprise widened David's eyes when he saw her.

She smiled. "Ye weren't expecting me."

"Nay, but I shouldn't be surprised to see ye."

Rory came down the stairs and crossed to where David sat and clasped his hand in greeting. "I figured ye wouldn't object to the aid of another agent."

"Ye figured right. We could use all the help we can on this mission."

Alex searched the room for another agent. "There's only David," she said to Rory. "Who will bring the weapons the rest of the way?"

"Ramsay will do it," Rory assured her.

Alex thought of the giant blacksmith and decided there was no one better to entrust with a wagon full of swords.

"Join me," David said, motioning to the empty chairs.

Alex sat down while Rory crossed to the keg and poured two tankards of ale, setting one in front of her. "Thank ye," she said quietly. Then she turned her attention to David. He sat up, looking like he was going to speak, but then he leaned back in his chair and took a long quaff of ale. Slamming down his empty cup, he said, "We're going to rob King Edward."

Rory chuckled into his ale. "Grand cracker, David. So, really what is our mission?"

David did not reply. He looked at Rory. Then he shifted his gaze and looked at Alex with the same challenging expression.

Confused, Alex broke the silence. "Does he have a contingent of men moving some coin?"

David stood, poured himself another ale, then turned back to her. "Actually, we're going to break into the King's palace in London."

Alex looked at Rory sidelong. He shook his head, assuring her that David was not in earnest, but she wasn't so sure. "Ye must be jesting."

David's humorless facade remained unaltered. "Rory can tell ye that I am not known to jest."

Rory narrowed his gaze on his friend. "Do ye mean to tell me that we're going to walk straight past King Edward and his court and all of his men and help ourselves to his treasury?"

David shook his head and sat back, a smile playing at his lips. He clearly enjoyed holding them in suspense. "The king, his household, and his treasury have moved to York. They are positioning themselves on the Scottish border. The truce is coming to an end."

Rory shrugged. "The king may not be in residence, but someone is. It hasn't been left empty."

"Ye're right. The palace of Westminster is far from empty. 'Tis full to the brim with philanderers and drunks."

"I do not understand," Alex said.

"Apparently, some things are beyond even Edward's control," David began. "Ye see, he could not appoint a proper keeper. The job passed into the hands of its hereditary keeper, a man by the name of John Francis Bigge who also holds the keepership of Fleet prison through his wife, Joan. At first John took little interest in his newfound responsibility. In fact, he installed a deputy named Martin Wilkins in his stead while he and his wife maintained their residence in the city. But in the absence of real authority, Martin quickly turned the king's palace into a den for sport."

"What kind of sport?" Alex asked.

"The salacious kind. And do ye ken what John did when he discovered Martin's debauchery?"

"He reprimanded him?" Alex offered.

David shook his head. "He packed his trunks, bid farewell to his wife, and joined Martin and all his scandalous companions in the palace." David leaned forward, a hungry glint in his eyes. "'Tis overrun with unsavory souls whose appetites for drink, women, and song are insatiable."

"What of the guard?" Rory asked.

"They, too, have joined the revelry, along with several monks from the neighboring abbey."

Rory sat back, allowing David's news sink in. "So, the keeper is careless and seeks not to guard the King's palace but to exploit it for what it's worth." He turned and smiled at Alex. "That changes everything."

Alex spoke up then. "But ye just said that Edward took his treasury with him to York. What is there left to steal?"

"Little remains of worth in the palace itself, but the king has treasure hidden away in the adjoining abbey."

Rory looked at David skeptically. "Surely the monks guard this treasure."

"As I said, many of the monks have proven to be incapable of resisting the temptations offered at court. In fact, the monks' disregard for their vows is how we came by this news. Word reached the abbot. He had no recourse but to send a man into the heart of the palace to be his eyes and ears."

Rory narrowed his eyes on David. "Ye're relying on only one man's account? Are ye certain this man is reliable?"

David looked at Rory with surprise. "Have ye ever known one of Scotland's agents to be unreliable?"

Rory shook his head. "Nay, but we've also never attempted anything so risky."

David sat back, an easy smile on his face. "Then rest assured. The man the abbot entrusted to spy on the workings of the king's palace is none other than yer older brother, Alec."

Rory threw his head back and whooped. "So, Alec is behind all this?"

David nodded. "The heist is his idea."

A slow smile crossed Rory's lips. Alec's involvement fueled his confidence. "Is he still in London?"

"Nay, he's made his excuses to his reveling companions and is awaiting us at the Harborage."

"What's the Harborage?" Alex asked.

Rory smiled at her. "Ye've not heard of the Harborage?"

"Nay."

"It would seem the abbot has been truly remiss," Rory said, reaching across to take her hand. "The Harborage is...well...ye'll see."

# Chapter Seventeen

Alex trudged through the dark woods, pulling her horse behind her. Thick underbrush obscured the ground, snagging at her tunic and cloak. Summer's sky warded off true night, allowing her to easily follow David, keeping his cloaked figure in sight.

"The Harborage is a safe haven," Rory said in a low voice behind her. "A place of meeting and rest for Scotland's agents. There is no road except that which we make ourselves."

Alex heard the stream before she saw it running alongside a line of tall slim pines, which rose high above the thicket. Then the underbrush began to thin out. Lush trees, silvery in the twilight, formed a canopy overhead. As the stream widened, the earth dipped in downward swells. Oak and pine gave way to tall, slim birch trees.

"I wonder why Abbot Matthew never told me about this place. He knows I have an appreciation for wild beauty." She scurried down the slope and through a copse of silver trees and stepped into an open glade alight with torch fire. Her mouth dropped open the instant after a man broke the surface of a glistening pool, clad in naught but his dripping wet hose. Fire and moonlight reflected off his wet muscles. She gasped, turning away, only for her gaze to settle on the shirtless form of another man seemingly asleep beneath a tree. She chuckled and turned to Rory. "It would seem the abbot sought to shield my maiden eyes." Then she stepped toward the gorgeous, dripping wet man. "Good evening, I'm Alex MacKenzie."

The man's black eyes locked with hers. A chill crept up her spine. His eyes shone like dark moons amid an empty pale sea. They were cold and emotionless. She waited for him to respond, but he only stared at her, penetrating her very soul. She swallowed hard and tore her gaze free from his hold. Her eyes traveled down his slick, lean shoulders and long, sinewy chest, still glistening with rivulets of water. Her gaze paused on the defined lines that crossed diagonally from his hips then disappeared beneath his low-slung, wet hose. Whoever he was, he was intense and beautifully made. Steeling her courage, her gaze returned to his stony yet exquisite face. She held her breath, waiting for him to speak, but then without a word, he turned and walked away from her.

Rory gently grabbed her arm. "My brother is a hard man to understand. I beg ye, do not be offended. He doesn't mean to be so callous. Wait here, please," he said before turning and following after who she now realized was Alec MacVie.

Rory charged after Alec. His brother had better have a good excuse for his rudeness. Not that Rory had expected Alec to greet Alex with conventional niceties. In fact, Alec had never been particularly nice. He was one of Rory's three older brothers. He also had one younger brother and an older sister. As siblings, they shared common traits. Each one possessed a fierce loyalty to family. They strove to live honorably, and none doubted their own self-worth, something instilled in their hearts by their parents. But beyond those deeply rooted convictions, they were all different—no one more so than Alec. He had always been quiet and reserved, even as a child, but it was not only Alec's temperament that set him apart from his other siblings. Alec had the Sight. His dreams revealed that which had already come to pass and that which had yet to be. But more than that, he could feel truth. He could feel another's pain.

Over the years, those who discovered Alec's abilities had called it a gift, although Rory had never understood their thinking. He likened it more to a burden. Alec moved through life, shielding himself from other's emotions. And his dreams seldom revealed anything other than heartbreak. Most often he saw death, destruction, or the wickedness in people's hearts. In fact, the day King Edward invaded Berwick, Rory and his sister had left the city limits to gather herbs. Alec had refused to join them. Their elder sister, Rose, pressed him again and again to say why he wouldn't join them. When he finally yielded, he confessed his dream from the night before. Rory could still remember the rare glimpse of feeling in Alec's eyes when he revealed that Berwick, their beloved city, had erupted into flame. Not believing Alec's dream contained an explicit meaning, Rose had begged him to join their walk, but Alec refused and went to the chapel to pray. That was where he was, in the chapel, when King Edward put the city under the blade and torch. Alec witnessed it all, the brutal slaughter of thousands—men, women, and children. None were spared, and only a few remained hidden. People were dragged from their homes and churches and butchered in the streets; not even the clergy was spared. Alec managed to escape the English blades, though he was, by no means, unscathed. After the massacre, he retreated further into himself, becoming quieter, harder.

Rory caught up to his brother. "Alec, explain yerself. That was rude—even for you."

Alec stopped and turned around. A flash of emotion crossed his usual mask of indifference—just for an instant. Someone who did not know Alec as well as Rory would have missed it. Immediately, tension flooded Rory's shoulders. It was never good when Alec lost control of his emotions.

"What is it?" Rory urged, his heart pounding.

Alec did not answer. He only looked at his brother, his black eyes cold, empty.

"Alec!"

"I have seen her face before," he said finally. "Last night in my dreams."

Fear surged through Rory. His mind went straight to the worst. "Please say ye didn't see her die."

"I didn't see her die," Alec said, his voice flat.

Rory expelled the breath he'd been holding.

"I saw her funeral."

He stumbled back, feeling as if he had just received a blow to the gut. He looked to his brother but received no comfort in his bleak eyes. His mind raced. He turned and stormed toward Alex.

"Come on, I'm taking ye home," Rory said, grabbing her by the arm.

She yanked free from his grasp. "What are ye talking about? Why would I go home?"

Rory raked his hand through his hair. Then he seized her, gripping her shoulders and looked her hard in the eye. "Because ye're going to die."

She pulled free and backed away. "Rory, what's come over ye?"

"Ye're going to die—My brother saw it."

"How could yer brother possibly know I'm going to die?"

"He has dreams, visions. I ken 'tis hard to believe, but he sees what is to come and senses what others cannot."

She froze, her heart quickening. "He has the Sight?" she said weakly.

Rory nodded to confirm.

Her mouth ran dry. She believed in the mysteries of the world and that the power of God moved through certain people. Alex turned and looked at Alec sitting alone beneath the tree. The moonlight made his straight, black hair gleam. It fell long, well past his shoulders and down his back. Having sensed her gaze, he lifted his head slightly. They locked eyes and a shiver crept up her back. He certainly had the feel of the fae. She crossed the glade, which shone silvery in the moonlight, and stood in front of him. He did not look at her, nor did he acknowledge her presence in anyway. Her eyes followed a path over the chiseled muscles of his bare shoulders. He was long and lean, less powerfully built than Rory, but she remembered how he had moved out of the water like something smooth and seamless, and yet so strong.

Slowly, she sat down beside him and studied his profile. His face was stony without appearing hard. She could describe him as impassive, but even that didn't quite capture his essence. He withstood her scrutiny without flinching, without an expressive display of any kind—as though he were a fine statue carved from beautiful stone—but there was nothing still about him. Alex could sense the whirl of his mind.

"Ye fight to contain it all inside of ye, don't ye," she whispered. "Ye don't want anyone to see."

She was not surprised when he continued to stare off into some distant place her own eyes could not see.

She tapped her hands on her knees. "So, ye're Alec, and I'm Alex—that could get confusing," she said, chuckling, but the sound of her awkward mirth trailed off into silence.

Finally, she blurted. "So ye saw me die."

This time the slightest movement caught her eye—an almost imperceptible shake of his head.

When he spoke, she started at the sound, having grown accustomed to his silence. "Not your death. Only your funeral."

"Do you believe I will die?"

"Yes," he said coolly. "We will all die one day."

She considered his words and realized he was telling her that he did not know.

He shifted his head, and they locked eyes. She froze beneath the weight of his black gaze. "Follow the command of yer own heart, Alex, just as ye've always done. It's brought ye this far, hasn't it?" Then he stood and strode off, disappearing into the woods.

She sat for a moment, feeling shaken to her core and yet oddly at peace.

Rory came to stand beside her. "Alec has a strange effect on everyone," he said knowingly.

She looked up at him, not having heard his approach. Confident words left her lips almost of their own bidding, as if her very heart spoke without consulting her mind. "My place is with ye, right here, fighting for Scotland."

Rory shook his head. "'Tis to dangerous."

"I know I may die, but so might we all. Our lives are in God's hands."

Rory shook his head harder. "Alex—"

"What if it had been ye, Rory?" She said, cutting him off. "What if Alec had dreamed about ye? Would ye go find a rock to hide beneath?"

Rory turned his back to her and raised his clenched fists above his head, growling before he turned back around. He released a long breath and met her gaze. "Nay," he said softly. "I would not."

She nodded and accepted his offered hand. "I have made my choice. I fight with ye."

He kissed her hand. "I will never seek to control ye, Alex." A smile broke the serious lines of his face. "Not that I could, even if I tried."

She reached up and cupped his cheek. "Thank ye for accepting me as I am," she said softly.

He pressed her hand against his heart. "I'm terrified something is going to happen to ye, and ye know how I feel about being afraid."

"Don't think about it. Run with me headlong into the fray. *Alba gu bràth*," she whispered.

He gently ran his fingers down her cheek. "*Alba gu bràth*," he said softly.

David cleared his throat, drawing their attention. "We have to discuss our plan."

Alex gestured toward the place in the woods where Alec had disappeared. "What about Alec? Will we not wait for his return?"

David shook his head. "He's told me everything we need to know, which is all the support he can provide. His work within the king's palace is not yet done. He cannot risk his true identity being discovered."

Alex and Rory joined David and two other men by the fire. "Alex, this is Paul and over there is Nick."

Alex smiled at Paul. He was the shirtless slumberer she had spied when first entering the glade. He appeared to be only a year or two older than she. His wet brown hair hung in soft curls around warm, dark eyes, which crinkled when he smiled in return. Nick, on the other hand, didn't even look up. His blond hair was also still wet from bathing. It was slicked back, and his eyes remained downcast while he ran a wet sharpening stone over his dirk.

"Ye all know where we're going tomorrow and what we're stealing, but now I am going to tell ye how," David said. "Alec has had the displeasure of meeting a man named Richard Ash. He calls himself a merchant but he's really no better than a peddler. According to Alec he once had a thriving trade in Flanders, but when King Edward withdrew from his holdings there, he left a slew of unpaid debts. The Flemish king sought compensation from the English merchants living inside his borders, claiming their profits and what remained of their goods. Richard returned to England with naught but the clothes on his back. Understandably, he was furious and went to the palace to seek compensation from the king, but, of course, he didn't find the king. Instead, he was greeted by disorder and debauchery—a scene that appealed to him straightaway. He easily charmed his way into the keeper's inner circle. But it was not only the wine and women that drew him to the palace. He saw opportunity. Since the beginning, he has been plotting how to rob the English king, gathering close a band of allies, which includes castle guards, monks from the neighboring abbey, and, fortunately for the cause, Alec MacVie, who knows the details of Richard's plan."

"So, this Richard has set the heist in motion, but we are going to take it over?" Rory asked.

"In a manner of speaking," David replied.

Rory shook his head. "But he was wronged by the king the same as us. I see no honor in stealing his prize."

"Do not give this man yer sympathies so quickly," David warned. "Alec has spent time in his company and has found little to recommend in his character. He is callous to those he calls friends, abusive to the servants remaining in the king's palace, and most disturbing to Alec is Richard's treatment of women. He steals for his own selfish gain, and Alec is convinced others will only suffer from his ill-gotten wealth."

Rory nodded. He had heard all he needed. Alec was the surest judge of character. Rory had no doubt that Richard was wicked to the core. "What is the plan?"

"Underneath the Chapel House of the abbey is a crypt where King Edward has stored countless treasures, plates, jewels, coin from Flanders and France."

Alex leaned forward eagerly. "So then, Richard plans to break into the crypt, and we must get there first."

David shook his head. "Richard has already broken into the crypt."

Rory threw his hands up. "Then he's already made off with the prize. Why are we wasting time with all this blather? Should we not run him down and seize it?"

"Calm yerself, Rory," David said, gesturing to Rory's tankard. "Have a sip of ale and listen. He's broken into the crypt, but he hasn't robbed it yet—not all of it anyway."

"I don't follow ye."

"He broke in last week and remains there still. Every day one of the monks waits by a hole they made in the Chapter House wall concealed by bushes. Every day he passes through one of the priceless treasures."

"But that's absurd," Paul said. "Does he not raise the risk of being caught?"

"'Tis arrogant but not as unreasonable as ye might first think. Ye see, he's afraid of being caught—not committing the act, mind ye, but when trying to turn the treasure into profit. Foreign coin cannot be used at market without raising questions of how he obtained it. And merchants are unlikely to barter for what would clearly be royal treasure. Neither Richard, nor any of his cronies, knows how to use what they've stolen. Their plan, at this point, is to hide the pieces until they figure it out."

Rory sat back in his chair. "Where are they hiding the pieces?"

"They're sinking the treasure to the bottom of rivers and ponds and burying it behind headstones."

"Considering they lack the connections we have, it's actually rather cunning," Alex said.

"And requires incredible patience, which is not often a virtue of one so willing to flout the law," Rory added.

David almost smiled. "I wouldn't accuse any us of being in possession of that virtue."

Alex laughed outright. "I suppose ye're right. We are a reactionary lot."

"And stubborn," Rory agreed.

"Not to mention feckless from time to time," Alex said, laughing.

"Let's put our foolhardiness to good use then," Rory said, raising his cup. "Let's go rob the king of England. *Alba gu bràth*."

Everyone but Nick raised their cups in kind. "*Alba gu bràth*."

"Now, get yer arses to bed," David said. "We wake before dawn. 'Tis two-day's hard ride to London." Then he dipped his head and turned, disappearing within the trees.

Paul stood and smiled. "This will be one to tell my grandchildren when I'm old and gray," he said, chuckling. Then he bowed at the waist to Alex. "I've heard of ye," he said. "'Tis a pleasure to meet the lady agent."

"The pleasure is mind," Alex said. She watched him retreat into a different portion of the woods.

Only Nick remained. Alex looked at him expectantly. She had yet to hear him say a word. She watched while he ran the sharpening stone slowly down the blade of his dirk one last time. Then he stood, and without even a glance in their direction, he crossed the glade and, like the others, disappeared between the trees.

"Don't pay Nick any heed," Rory said. "He's a good agent, his loyalty to Scotland unquestioned, but he's hard, ruthless even. A part of me understands why. His family, his wife and three children, were burned alive in their home during the massacre."

Alex gasped, her heart suddenly aching for Nick.

Rory nodded. "'Tis unthinkable, I ken, but his pain and fury have blackened his soul. Meeting Nick helped soothe the same beast within me. After my parents and sister were slain, I desired vengeance, blood. Now, I fight only for freedom."

Alex scanned the woods. "They all left in different directions. Where have they gone?"

Rory pointed to the sky. "Into the trees. The Harborage is our haven, remember? A place for us to rest without fear. We've built platforms within tree branches. They are concealed by canopies of leaves and underbrush."

Alex frowned. "Abbot Matthew will hear from me on this matter. All this while an Eden has existed, and I've been denied because I'm a woman. 'Tis unjust. I work just as hard as anyone else. Do I not deserve a bath in a lovely, moonlit pool?"

Rory smiled. "I for one think ye do. In fact, why don't ye avail yerself of that luxury now?" He gestured toward the empty pool, which glistened in the moonlight on the other side of the glade.

She gazed at the inviting water and started toward it. "I believe I shall."

"I will keep watch," he said.

The corner of her mouth lifted into a sensual smile. "Actually, I insist ye watch." She boldly turned to face him and eased her tunic over her head. She met his gaze and stood for a moment, allowing him to feast his gaze upon her body, clad only in her kirtle. Then she removed the thin barrier and stood before him naked in the moonlight.

He looked at her hungrily, his eyes slowly traveling over every inch of her bare flesh. "Ye're magnificent."

She smiled and threw her kirtle at him, then dove into the water. Icy currents swept over her skin. She squealed when she surfaced. "It bites," she said.

Rory looked down at her. "So do I."

His words shot through her, igniting her body with warmth despite the frigid pool. Her heart quickened. She licked her lips as she took in his large frame, his penetrating gaze. She promised herself, in that moment, that one day she would again know the feel of his hands on her body.

But what if she didn't have one day more?

Alec's prophesy trumpeted in her mind. What if she was going to die? Her heart quaked, but not with fear. She was not afraid to die for the cause. Her heart trembled for that which she feared most—regret. What if she were to die without ever lying in Rory's arms? She sucked in a sharp breath and dove beneath the surface.

Rory crouched down beside the water's edge and waited for her to appear again. She emerged directly in front of him, the surface of the pool lapping her waist. Water sluiced off her firm, proud breasts. His mouth watered at the sight of her taut peaks.

As if of their own accord, her arms flew around his neck. "I will have ye now, Rory."

He pulled away to look into her eyes, which gleamed with near feverish intensity. "But...what about your duty?" he said.

"Nay! I will not think of duty right now. My whole life I have thought of little else." She cupped his cheeks, bringing his lips a breath away from her own. "What if this is all we have? This moment. This night. I want yer hands on my body."

His heart pounded. Hunger gripped him like nothing he had ever felt before. He brushed her lips with a kiss—the barest whisper of a caress. Then he plunged his hands into the water and cradled her up through the air, icy water soaking his clothes. "I'm going to make yer body quake," he promised and carried her toward the trees.

High in the treetop, a canopy of leaves hid her naked body, even from the stars above. Only Rory could feast upon her luscious curves. Her body was both soft and strong. He ran his hand down the gentle slope of her waist, over her hip and down her long sleek leg. She wrapped her arms around his neck, slowly pulling him closer, her lids half-closed, heavy with desire. He ran the backs of his fingers gently down her cheek. Then he crushed his lips to hers. She groaned, clinging to him, her tongue stroking his.

"Take this off," she cried out, tearing at his tunic.

He whisked the fabric over his head and winced as her nails dug into his back. He grabbed her hands and pinned them over her head with one hand while he swept his other hand over her breast. With his palm he gently caressed her nipple. Then he lowered his mouth, His hot breath teasing her hard peak. He stroked it with his tongue, forcing a gasp from her lips. Then he seized it gently between his teeth, and she cried out. He drew the point deeper into his mouth and suckled her while she writhed beneath him, soft moans escaping her lips. She twisted to release her hands from his steel grip. Still, he held her, trapping her while he slowly caressed her hip and smoothed over the dip of her stomach. Then his fingers brushed the soft curls, and he cupped her mound.

"Let me go," she cried. "I want to touch ye. I want to feel yer body."

"In a minute, love," he said softly. Then he held her gaze while he gently pushed her thighs apart. He trailed his fingers slowly from her knee, up the inside of her thigh, his touch soft as a whisper. He paused just as he reached the very heat of her. She bucked her hips, her eyes pleading.

"Please, Rory," she cried.

He watched the agony of desire twist her features as his touch barely grazed her flesh.

Again, her hips bucked against his hand, her body demanding more. He leaned over and seized her lips the instant he deepened his touch. Her body, hot and wet, contracted around him, and he stroked her, bringing her higher and higher. Then her eyes flew open. "Rory, I want ye to make me yers," she cried.

He groaned, releasing her hands. She came onto her knees and pulled on the waist of his hose, freeing his hard length. He pushed her back onto the platform and positioned himself between her legs. Then slowly, so slowly, he entered her. Her tight sheath constricted around him. She was so tight. He held his breath as he stretched her wider until he filled her. She wound her arms firmly around him, her face buried against his neck, and slowly he started to thrust. Her hips met his, her body slick with sweat. She gripped him. He thrust harder, then faster. Her breath filled his ears. Her pounding heart beat against his chest. She wrapped her legs around his waist, and pulled down on him, meeting his hard thrusts with furious demand. She seized, as a cry tore from her lips, then she shuddered and quaked in his arms. He drove deeper, her rapture tearing through him, bringing his own body toward exquisite pain, which suddenly released as wave after wave of pleasure shot through him.

# Chapter Eighteen

B ent low, Alex quickly climbed from the riverboat onto the King's bridge. She stayed close behind Rory as they hugged the palace's inner wall. Turret's loomed overhead bearing the king's colors. They came to a break in the wall.

"Wait," David hissed behind her. She and Rory stopped, hunkering down against the wall.

"Wasn't that the gate?" David whispered as he pointed to the map Alec had drawn. Paul and Nick sidled up behind them.

"I think it was," Nick whispered.

Rory grabbed the map and shook his head. "'Tis the second gate. We must circle around first. "Then we'll have a straight shot into the abbey grounds."

David nodded and rolled up the parchment, then motioned for Rory to go. Alex stayed right behind Rory as they continued around the wall.

At the next gate, Rory turned and looked at her. "Remember," he whispered, "this is the most vulnerable stretch. The abbey's infirmary is to the left. Alec said the monks who remain there are loyal to Edward, but seldom leave. Move quickly."

She nodded and turned to David. "This is it," she said.

Rory raced through the gate. She followed right behind. Her eyes darted to the left. Torch fire lit the glass windows in the infirmary. She pushed harder, following the narrow path, which cut through the abbey's cemetery. Up ahead, she could see the circular design of the Chapter House. Rory led them away from the garden entrance, knowing that was where

Richard and his cronies had made their hole, and instead followed the cemetery to the dormitory.

Alec had assured them that at that late hour the rest of the
monks would be in the palace's great hall well into their cups.
Alex held her breath as Rory slowly pushed the door open. Inside was dark. She dared not breathe as she silently crossed the
floor, expecting the hand of a holy man to snake out and grab
her arm at any moment. Then she froze. A soft snore rattled
from the far corner of the dark room. Rory seized her hand,
and David grabbed her arm from behind. They stood rooted to the floor for several moments. Her heart pounded, almost drowning out the sound of the sleeping monk. Then Rory eased forward. She followed behind, waiting to hear Rory's
fingertips graze the far wall.

A soft tap sent a surge of relief through her. She heard his
careful exploration of the wall and knew when he had found
the door by the quiet click of the handle. He eased it open.
She held her breath as candlelight from the cloister invaded the
dormitory. She glanced back at the monk now clearly visible in
his narrow bed.

Her heart pounded in her ears as she followed Rory into
the hallway with David, Paul, and Nick at her heels. They circled halfway around the cloister, and just as Alec promised,
there was the sacristy, beside which was the only entrance to
the crypt beneath the Chapter House. Resisting the urge to
race forward, she kept pace behind Rory. Their practiced steps
made no din as they crossed to the door. Rory opened it and
darted inside. Torch fire lit the dark stairwell. She descended
behind Rory. Glancing back, she saw David and Paul right behind her. But Nick stayed at the top of the stairs to guard the

entrance. They circled around three times. Then Rory stopped and turned. He motioned for her to turn. She felt him check that her sword was secure. Then he cupped her cheeks and kissed her hard on the lips before he started back down the stairs.

Her heart raced. This was it. Three more turns and they would reach the drop into the crypt where royal treasure and Richard Ash awaited.

RICHARD ASH'S CHEST tightened as he once again scanned his strangely opulent surroundings. The crypt beneath the abbey floor had been transformed from a dark, empty stone chamber to a glittering treasure house that surpassed even his wildest dreams. For nearly a week he had spent night and day beneath the Chapter House, and still he marveled at the glorious sight. The stone arched ceilings and carved faces of tortured saints might have appeared sinister, but as he gazed upon the glittering jewels, chests of coin, rolls of rich velvet, he felt like weeping. The only way down to the crypt was a long, winding stairwell next to the sacristy, but the stairs did not reach the floor. They ended abruptly, making a drop off nearly the length of two men from the last stair to the crypt floor.

He wrapped the cloak he wore tighter around his shoulders against the creeping chill, which signaled night had fallen. Still, the cold could not penetrate his newly acquired thick velvet robe. He swept the purple fabric with an elegant flourish, admiring the rich color. Commoners were forbidden to wear purple. For his crime, he could be sent to the stocks for weeks. He stroked the soft ermine fur, which lined the edges of the cloak and closed his eyes against the intense pleasure, moaning aloud, his fingertips tingling. His eyes flew open as the experience overwhelmed his senses. He took his hand away from the fur to catch his breath, but then his eyes caught sight of the rings lining his fingers, making his heart pound harder. Each ring held a stone the size of a plump blackberry. He straightened out his arm, admiring how the jewels glinted in the torchlight. For the first time in his life, he smiled at his small, thin fingers with pride. They looked stronger—the hands of a man who answered to no one. His smile curled into a sneer. If only his father could see him.

His father had never believed in him. When the larger boys walloped him in the streets for sport, he'd return home bruised and bloodied, only to have his father beat him as punishment for his weakness. His father, his teacher, his priest and everyone else for that matter, never believed he would accomplish anything, but Richard soon learned to work their contempt to his advantage. It was easy to surprise those who expected nothing from him. This was how he rose to power right under his father's nose, stealing his best customers right out from under him. Because his father never truly saw Richard, he never saw him coming—for who would have expected a weakling, a disappointment, to become a wealthy merchant. In no time, his father was penniless and begging Richard for help.

"Anything," his father had pleaded. "I will take anything ye give me."

And Richard had complied by giving his father an extra helping of misery.

His mother, who was naught but a drunk, had taken to humping the neighbor. Richard led his father to the very room in which they were fornicating. Keeping his eyes trained on his father's face, he threw the door open and watched. Confusion pinched his father's features. Then surprise widened his eyes, followed by a rage that shook his jowls, but his father had been too broken to act on his fury. An instant later, his face crumpled.

A chuckle bubbled up Richard's throat as it always did when he remembered his father's utter humiliation.

Witnessing his father's pain had always been Richard's greatest victory; however, that sweet memory was quickly moving to a close second behind the present moment—Himself, standing in purple velvet, surrounded by more riches than he ever dreamed existed. If only the lads on Westcheap Street could see him now.

And he had earned it all—down to the last penny.

King Edward had abused his power in Flanders and ruined everything for Richard. It had been so easy to prey on the Flemish who were naturally more trusting than the English. Instead of interpreting his small stature as a weakness, he was met with goodwill and pity. Once again, he was able to surprise people, making them so easy to cheat. A few sweet words from him, and suddenly they were emptying their coffers, buying what they did not need.

But all that came to an end after King Edward beguiled them all.

Richard clenched his hands into tight fists when he remembered how swiftly the Flemish king had exacted his revenge. Overnight, Richard found himself stripped of his wealth and belongings, sailing home to England, a failure. But he never doubted that he would once again rise to the top. And at long last, he had done just that. He proudly surveyed the king's treasure.

Nay, it was his treasure.

He closed his eyes and lost himself in his newfound favorite pastime. He imagined all the wonderful things he would do with his riches. He could not only have his pick of the best whores, but he could also make them his slaves. As soon as the heist was finished, he would cheat the men working with him. They were all so stupid, they would never know they hadn't gotten their fair share.

With that in mind, one of those fools should soon drop a sack down the hole they had made through the thick rock wall of the Chapter House then down into the crypt, and he still had yet to make the day's final pick. He narrowed his choice to either a gold plate encircled with rubies and emeralds or a sleek dirk. Picking up the blade, he held it in his hand. It was short and light with an ornate hilt, encrusted by a rainbow of small gems. He shoved the dirk into his satchel, deciding to keep it rather than hide it away to be bartered when they found a willing merchant. Clasping the plate, he looked up at the hole, and from the corner of his eye caught a flash of black soar through the air. He whirled around just as two masked figures landed on the stone floor. Richard dropped the bejeweled plate and screamed, covering his head with his hands while he scurried to the far corner.

Alex froze. Her mouth agape, she stared at Richard Ash—or at least what she could see of him—through the eyeholes in her mask. He crouched against the wall, mewling and blubbering for mercy, shielding his face and head with his arms as if he were being pummeled by large fists.

"P...p...please, don't hurt me. Take it. Take all of it. Just...just don't hurt me," he wailed. Then he howled and rolled around on the ground, knocking into a large bowl with a gold plate for a lid. The plate slid to one side and the contents sloshed on the floor, releasing a horrific stench. Clearly, Richard had just disturbed his week-old chamber pot. She gagged and covered her mouth with her hand, but Rory grabbed her arm and motioned for her to fill one of her large satchels. Taking shallow breaths through her mouth, she filled her first bag. Rory tossed it, along with the one he had filled, onto the platform above where Paul and David waited, both wearing hooded masks. Alex carried on filling another sack, every now and then glancing at Richard's pathetic figure still pleading and blubbering and now steeped in his own waste. She certainly did not need the small sword strapped to her back or the length of rope tied loosely around her waist to restrain him if he had decided to challenge them. His fear and cowardice were restraint enough. She shook her head, still astounded by his total surrender of control, while she grabbed three large, gold platters and several bags of coin and put them into another bag. Because they were too heavy to toss, Rory tied one end of the rope to the bag and tossed the other end up to Paul or David, she could not tell, and together, the men pulled the heavy bag up to the landing. She wondered if Nick could hear Richard's desperate pleas at the top of the stairwell.

She had one last satchel to fill. She hurried to a pile of coin and began stuffing it into the bag. Richard's blubbering had grown to convulsing sobs as he pleaded with the Almighty for his unworthy life to be spared. Not far from where he lay, she spotted a gold plate with enormous jewels. Carefully stepping around the excrement-smeared floor, she leaned down to pick it up the instant before Richard lunged and seized her mask, ripping it off.

"What kind of fool do you take me for?" he spat, pressing the tip of a dirk to her throat.

She sucked in a sharp breath; she knew his face!

A glint suddenly lit his puffy eyes. "Lady Alexandria MacKenzie—I can't believe it's you." He grinned, showing rotted, black teeth.

Rory whirled around, his ears ringing with the sound of Richard's voice speaking Alex's name. Fury seized him when he saw her face unmasked and a knife to her throat. He grabbed a goblet from the ground and launched it at the man's head. An instant later, Richard's eyes rolled behind his lids, and he crumpled to the ground, unconscious.

"What the hell is going on?" David shouted.

Rory ignored David and rushed to Alex's side. "Are ye all right? Did he hurt ye?"

"He knew yer name," David shouted. "How is that possible?"

"Shut up," Rory snapped.

Alex gripped the sides of her head and her breathing became ragged. "He came through my village last spring, peddling his goods. He tried to cheat my people, so I ran him off."

"Damnation," Rory cursed.

"Get him. Bind his feet," David urged. "We'll pull him up."

Rory nodded, then looked back at Alex. "It will be all right. I promise ye."

She took a deep breath and nodded. He could see the initial shock leave her eyes and her mettle return. She untied the rope around her waist and handed it to Rory. "I'll hold his feet."

After binding Richard's feet, Rory dragged their putrid captive toward the platform. Tossing the other end of the rope to David, Rory warned, "He's a foul one."

Once they pulled Richard out of the crypt, David dropped the rope back down. Alex seized it and Paul whisked her up to the landing. She tossed the end down to Rory and a moment later all four agents began to carry the sacks of treasure up the stairs to where Nick waited, keeping guard at the sacristy door. Then Rory and David returned to grab Richard.

"What are ye doing?" Nick growled when they came up the stairs, dragging Richard behind them, his head knocking against the stone steps.

"The plan was to leave him in the bleeding crypt," Nick cried.

Rory whirled around and snapped. "He saw Alex's face."

Nick threw his hands up. "She was supposed to be masked."

"Enough," Rory snapped. "'Tis too late to change what happened. We are running out of time."

They hauled the treasure and Richard farther around the cloisters, away from the dormitory and the slumbering monk, and out into the courtyard to the stables and filled a wagon.

Everyone climbed onto the back of the wagon, while Rory finished hitching the horses. Then he took the reins and urged the beasts forward. Cutting back through the cemetery, he passed through the gate to the palace grounds, coming face to face with two monks returning to the abbey.

The holy men's eyes widened with fear at the sight of the masked rebels. Then they turned on their heels and started to run toward the palace doors, but Nick leapt from the wagon, tackling them both to the ground.

"Do not kill them," Rory cried as he, too, jumped to the ground.

Nick squatted above the monks, holding their faces in a fierce grip. "Remember yer vows," he hissed. Then he released them and started backing up toward the wagon. "Go to the chapel and beg God for forgiveness."

The monks lay on the ground, frozen with fear.

"Now," Nick growled.

They scrambled to their feet, then tripped on their robes in their haste and stumbled to the ground. They shot a look back at the wagon.

Nick unsheathed his sword. The sight forced whimpers from their lips as they once more found their footing and raced toward the abbey, disappearing through the gate.

Rory had no doubt they were headed to the chapel to pray. "Hurry," he called to Nick from the wagon. As soon as Nick jumped back on, Rory snapped the reins. They surged forward. He circled around the palace outer wall to the King's Bridge and down to the Thames. They moved the treasure, splitting the weight between two riverboats. Then Paul and Nick dragged Richard into their boat and took up their paddles, heading downriver with Rory, Alex, and David following behind in the second boat.

Alex dug her paddle deep into the water, then pulled the wood free from the current, only to plunge it back in an instant later. Again and again, she strained to gain as much speed as possible. They needed to clear the city limits to the wooded bank, where Alec awaited with more wagons and horses. Her mind raced. She still could not believe it. She had been seen. Not only seen—she had been recognized, and in connection with the robbery of the King's palace. Her worst fear had come true. Surely, King Edward's wrath would rain down upon the whole MacKenzie clan.

# Chapter Nineteen

# Back at Luthmore

"Corc, ye need to take the bread," Mary said, a crusty loaf in her outstretched hands.

Corc smiled. "Like I told ye already, the ladies in the village keep me fat as butter," he said, while patting his trim belly. "Give that to someone who needs it."

Mary stood her ground. "Ye've hardly an inch around yer middle to spare. Listen to me, Corc. We do this dance every time Alex is away when I know for a fact ye accept the bread when she does the rounds. Helen told me so. Please, take it. Don't make me drag Alex from her sick bed." Mary looked down the lane and saw Helen waving from her door.

Corc nudged the bread away. "Give it to Helen," Corc replied. "Look at all the wee ones she has. To be sure, she needs it more than I do."

Mary was about to give in, but then William, who was assisting her with rounds, drew close and whispered the secret to sway Corc's mind.

Mary winked at Will, then turned to Corc. "Please," she said sweetly. "As a favor to me."

A gummy smile, stretching from ear to ear, lit Corc's face. "When ye put it like that, ye know I cannot refuse ye," he said, taking the bread.

Mary laughed and threw her arms around Corc's neck, pressing a kiss to his cheek.

The sound of pounding hooves drew her attention. She pulled away from Corc and spotted Gavin galloping toward them. He reined in his horse in front of Corc's cottage and reached out a hand for her, saying, "The MacLeod's colors were spotted on the road. His arrival is imminent."

Mary nodded and took Gavin's hands. He lifted her into the saddle in front of him, then raced to the keep. Riding straight to the doors of the great hall, he lowered her to the ground. Without pause, she hurried inside, calling Rosie to her. Together they hastened to Mary's chambers and quickly yanked her work clothes off. Mary stepped into a fresh kirtle and fitted the straps over her shoulders a moment before Rosie pulled a tunic over her head. Both women were panting as Mary stepped into her surcote.

"Hurry," she said to Rosie as the maid started to adorn Mary's head. Deftly pinning a second veil over her wimple, Rosie stepped back and declared, "Ye're presentable. Go, Mary!"

Gasping for air, Mary raced from the room, down the stairs and beyond the screen into the great hall and straight into Adam's arms.

"It will be all right," he soothed.

"I know," she said. "I just have to catch my breath and find my composure." She closed her eyes and breathed, allowing herself to lean on Adam for support. Then she took a deep breath and stepped back. "Thank ye."

Adam took her arm and led her in front of the high table. "Michael has told me everything. I understand the McLeod chieftain is a potential threat. I've instructed Gavin to gather the guard and have a portion of them present here in the hall and the remainder in the courtyard. Robert, Timothy, and Finlay will greet the laird at the gate and escort his party inside." Then he turned to face her. "If ye will have me, I will stand with ye, Mary."

Swallowing the knot that had lodged in her throat, Mary looked up to Adam and nodded. "I would be most grateful."

Emboldened by Adam's presence at her side, Mary closed her eyes once more and forced herself to calm down. She could handle the MacLeod.

The door opened. Finlay, Robert and Timothy led the way to the high table. Then they stepped aside, allowing Gordon MacLeod, and his son, Eudard, to stand in front of Mary. The other MacLeod warriors, less than half a dozen in number, remained in the rear of the hall. Following Alex's example, Mary stood tall and looked the chieftain in the eye. As he stood before the high dais, she was surprised by how tall Gordon and Eudard were.

"Good morrow," Gordon said, dipping his head to Mary. His cold eyes belied the smile that curved his lips. At his side, Eudard also dipped his head, but he eyed Adam with open hostility.

"We have come to pay the lady of the keep a visit. We bring with us gifts of grain and seed." The MacLeod narrowed his eyes on Mary. Then his gaze shifted to Adam. At length, he turned and took a few steps toward Robert and Timothy, and with a look of open disdain, he surveyed them from head to toe, before turning back to face Mary. "But it would seem she already has visitors."

Adam stepped forward then. "Ye're correct, Laird MacLeod. I am Sir Adam Lennox." Then he motioned to

Robert. "There stands Sir Robert Gow and Sir Timothy Cunningham. We are friends of the MacKenzie clan."

"As are we," Gordon snapped, his eyes narrowing on Adam. "Lady Alexandria will attest to this. Where is she? Why has she not welcomed us herself."

"She is unwell," Mary said. Despite her nervousness, her voice rang out strong and steady.

The MacLeod gave pause. Although he tried to conceal it, Mary noticed the hint of smile that curved his lips the instant before his brow furrowed with false concern.

"I pray her condition is not grave."

"I assure ye, it is not," Mary said.

The MacLeod cleared his throat and started to back away. "Given ye have several guests to accommodate already and the present concern over yer lady's health, we will not lean on yer hospitality any further. Ye'll find the grain and seed in the courtyard. We shall keep the lady Alexandria in our prayers." He wet his lips and eyed Mary, canting his head to the side as if seeing her for the first time. "We shall leave ye, for now," he said, then he bowed and turned on his heel and stormed from the great hall with Eudard keeping pace behind him.

Mary expelled a slow breath. Only when the door closed behind the MacLeod did her knees start to tremble. She reached out for Adam. He swept her into his arms to keep her from falling.

"Lady Mary," he exclaimed. "Are ye unwell?"

She closed her eyes for a moment and rested her head against his shoulder. "I will be fine. Just nerves," she said.

He smiled down at her. "Ye were brilliant. When Alex is well enough to receive visitors, I will tell her myself how masterfully ye handled Laird MacLeod."

Mary blushed and cast her gaze downward, unable to bear the exquisite beauty of Adam's warm, green eyes. "Thank ye," she whispered. Then the greed she witnessed in the MacLeod's eyes came unbidden to her mind.

Please, Alex, she prayed. Hurry home.

"SO WHAT IF HE SAW YER face?" David said. "He can do little with that knowledge."

"He knows who I am," Alex said, urging the other agents to understand the significance of what had occurred. "King Edward's vengeance will be taken not just against me but against my clan."

"God's blood," David cursed, pacing back and forth.

David stopped abruptly and turned around. "There's naught to be done. We'll have to kill him," he said, gesturing to the blindfolded and gagged man, sprawled out on the grass across the glade.

Alex's eyes widened in alarm. Nothing mattered more to her than her people. Still...murder? There had to be another way.

To her relief Rory turned to David and said, "No one is killing anybody."

David raked his hand through his hair. "But ye just spelled out in no uncertain terms that the situation is dire. Surely, ye will not sacrifice the wellbeing of so many for the tainted soul of this rotter."

Rory pulled Alex close. Although to the rest of their company he knew she appeared calm, he could tell by the flush of her skin and the slight crease in her brow how worried she really was. He knew she feared not for herself but for her people. "We'll stick to the code laid out by my brother, Jack, and Abbot Matthew. We're thieves not murderers. If we cross this line, then we are no better than King Edward himself."

"I remember a time when ye wouldn't have thought twice about killing the likes of him," Nick snapped.

"And I thank the Lord everyday I've learned some sense since then."

David let out a slow breath, then shrugged. "Mayhap we worry for naught. We forget that Alex is actually Lady Alexandria. 'Tis the word of a lady against a thieving peddler."

Alex shook her head. "Ye're wrong. 'Tis the word of an Englishman against that of a Scotswoman. My title lost its value the moment the English king invaded."

"Then ye must go into hiding," David said.

"And leave my people alone and vulnerable?" Alex replied. "If the king's men come seeking the truth and discover I fled, that would only prove my guilt."

Alec stepped forward then, speaking for the first time. "If ye do not run, ye'll be taken and put in the tower—ye'll die."

"Then I shall die," Alex snapped, meeting his hard, black eyes. "I will not be a coward."

"Wait," Rory said, drawing their gazes. "She won't die." Then he turned to face Alec. "But she will have a funeral."

"What are ye talking about?" Alex said. Rory and Alec had locked eyes, and she noticed for the first time a smile playing about the edges of Alec's lips.

"Ye said ye did not see her death," Rory said softly. "Only her funeral."

"Ye want me to pretend to die?" she gasped.

Rory reached for her and cupped her cheek. "Yer people believe ye've already taken ill, remember?"

She nodded, recalling her last words to Mary, advising her not to let anyone into her chamber, including Michael and William. That was only six days ago. She could guess at Rory's plan. They would sneak back into her chamber and have Mary and Rosie spread the word that her fever had worsened, and she had caught the pox Rory initially argued had been too severe an illness to fake. Fear of contagion would allow them to continue the charade until it was fitting to say that the illness had robbed her of her life. Given her options—the risk of being taken to the tower to meet her actual death, fleeing and allowing her people to suffer the wrath of King Edward, or killing a man in cold blood—pretending she had died appeared to be the best course of action.

She turned to Alec. His dark, blank eyes held hers. Her heart heavy, she said, "It would appear as though ye did indeed foresee the future. I'm to have a funeral after all."

# Chapter Twenty

Alex sat astride her mount on the brink of the cliffs of Tor-na Doon. In the distance, Luthmore sat swaddled by sloping moors and a ribbon of stone. Despite its true, towering height, it somehow appeared small and fragile. Mist clung to the walls, drifting up from the surrounding moat, pacifying the stone, which labored day after day to contain the life within its hard embrace, all the laughter and tears, joy and sorrow. Countless souls had drawn their first breath within those walls and some their last. Her mother and father had lived and died there. Her own girlish squeals of delight used to ricochet off the towering ceilings of the great hall while she chased Mary around the lines of trestle tables. She clutched the reins hard between her fingers while her aching sorrow grew.

She had become a woman there, striding purposefully down the halls and across the moors of Luthmore. She had been taught to care for her people—to give her back to the plough, her shoulder to cushion their tears, her will to protect them, and her heart to love them all.

But her soul did not reside within that distant stone—not anymore, mayhap it never had. Her restless spirit had always looked outward. Still, for her people, she would have silenced the wolf within her and forever put her duty first. But now duty demanded she leave her clan.

Rory brought his horse alongside hers and rested his strong hand gently against her back. She closed her eyes, banishing the image of Luthmore castle from view. Shifting in her saddle, she opened her eyes and gave herself over to Rory. Brows drawn, a sad smile curved his lips. She grabbed his hand, pulling the backs of his fingers to her lips, which were pressed together in a thin line to contain her heartache. He reached for her, but she brought her other hand between them in a silent bid for him to wait. She had to speak, but first she needed to fight the turmoil within her heart. Peace and acceptance awaited her; she could feel their promise, but they had to be earned. With both hands, she clasped his and kissed his roughened knuckles. Then she uncurled his fingers to feel his hard, calloused palm against her cheek. Drawing a measured breath, she drank in the comfort of his touch.

"My whole life," she began, her lips quivering, "I have given my heart to my people." She closed her eyes against the wave of emotion that tightened her chest at the mention of her kin. She allowed the pain to wash over her, but she did not nurture it or cling to what was. "And then one night, I asked a rebel to undress me in a dark forest while the thrill of the cause coursed through my veins. I looked into his sky-blue eyes and found myself unexpectedly in their exquisite depths." Those same blue eyes burned soul-deep as she continued. "A piece of my heart will always reside in Luthmore. But my soul lives in ye, Rory MacVie: my own rebel thief. I love ye, ye and no other. I—"

The rebel thief stole once more—this time the very words from her lips as his own claimed hers with a force that burst the well of emotion building within her heart, her soul—all for him.

He pulled her onto his lap, his lips never leaving hers, and kissed her with crushing strength, his heart pounding. Then he tore away and stared deep into her violet eyes, still brimming with a flood of unshed tears. "I love ye, Alex, simply and wholly. Ye're my life. I care not where we go or of the struggles we face. I ask only one thing from ye on this day, and never more will I ask another. Just take me with ye. Wherever ye go, I go with ye."

She grabbed his tunic, nodding fiercely. "We are one, ye and I."

He cupped her cheeks and crushed his lips against hers. He could barely draw breath as he struggled to contain the enormity of his emotion. So great was his love, he imagined it might break through the surface of his skin, shooting streaks of fiery passion from his very soul. She clung to him, breathless, her heart pounding against his chest, urging his own to beat faster, to want more. Rory dismounted and, bringing an arm beneath her legs, he cradled her, laying her on the ground. Their lips moved in an erratic dance of longing and love. She gripped his back, pulling the full weight of his body onto her. His strength surrounded her. She stroked his wide back, down to his tapered waist. Running her thumbs along his waist, she lifted her hips, her body seeking release.

He rested his weight on his elbow, slowly easing her tunic past her knees, then to her waist. She spread her legs wide for him. Covering her once more, she cried out when he entered her—a chord of sinful harmony blessed by love's admission. He lost himself to the ache and longing that filled him, to the love that threatened to consume him. Even the rock beneath them, as old as the world's very beginnings, reveled in the coupling of two bodies, two souls so perfectly matched.

ALEX ROUNDED THE NARROW stairs, lit by the torch Rory carried behind her. Reaching above her head, her fingers disappeared into shadow and grazed slatted wood. She flattened her palms against the trap door, ready to push. But the door swung open, and the tip of a blade came into view.

"Och, Mary and all the Saints be praised. 'Tis ye," Rosie exclaimed. The sword in her hand clattered to the ground as she grabbed Alex by the arms and yanked her up the rest of the stairs and into a fierce embrace.

"Rosie, I can hardly breathe," Alex laughed.

"Leave something of her for me to hug," she heard Mary say excitedly.

Rosie released her, and straightaway, Mary seized her. "Ye cannot imagine how I've missed ye, dear cousin." Mary said. "I ken ye weren't gone long, but so much happened in yer absence."

"Indeed, it did," Alex whispered, folding her arms around her beloved Mary. An acute pang cut straight through Alex's heart. How would she get on without Mary? Then the ache within her grew when she considered how Mary would get on without her. Alex took a deep breath to steady her racing heart. She knew her cousin would be heartbroken, but she also believed in Mary's quiet strength. She would become a great Lady of Luthmore—better even than Alex, for Mary possessed all of Alex's compassion and goodness but none of her rebellion.

"I have missed ye too," Alex said.

Rory cleared his throat, drawing everyone's gaze.

"Welcome back," Rosie said, stepping forward to relieve Rory of his now doused torch.

Mary dipped in a low curtsy before saying. "Ye're both back and in good health. How much longer must we carry on with this pretense?"

Rosie stepped forward. "I can go now and announce that yer fever has broken. Then at least Michael and William can come and visit ye. They've both been hounding me night and day to see ye. I refused them as ye said to, although I know it hurt William's heart to be denied. Ye're going to have to hug him with all yer might when he arrives."

Mary's face brightened. "Go now, Rosie. Make the announcement and fetch Will."

"Wait, Rosie," Alex blurted.

Rosie turned around and looked at Alex with brows raised. "Why?" Then she smiled. "Och, of course!" She stormed at Rory, shooing him away. "Back down the stairs with ye. Ye'll have to fetch a horse somehow and make a show of yer return to Luthmore through the front gate."

Rory threw his hands up. "Whoa, Rosie. There's something ye don't know."

Alex's chest tightened. She tried to speak, to tell Rosie that she couldn't go downstairs and tell the clan she was on the mend—not when she was about to feign her death. Her stinging tears could no longer be denied. She covered her face with her hands and dropped to her knees, her heart already mourning the loss of her family and beloved friends. Mary's arms came around her shoulders. Alex turned toward her cousin, resting her face against her chest while Mary rocked her. "There, there, love."

"What is the matter with her?" Rosie demanded of Rory.

"Our last mission did not go entirely as planned," Rory said.

At length, Alex garnered her strength and curbed her tears. Rory shifted the chairs around and made room for everyone to sit by the hearth, and while Alex held Rosie's hand to her left and Mary's to her right, Rory began his account of their latest mission. "We robbed the king's palace in London."

Mary's eyes widened with alarm. "Ye must be jesting!"

Mary and Rosie both looked at Alex expectantly.

Pressing her lips into a thin line, her only answer was to nod her head.

Rosie fanned herself with her free hand. "I feel faint."

"Steady now, Rosie," Rory said, his voice firm. "I need ye to be strong. Something has occurred that cannot be undone."

Alex alternated between soothing Mary and then Rosie while Rory finished recounting the details of the heist. "Nick and Paul carried on to Haddington with the treasure while Alex and I raced back here."

For a moment, Rosie and Mary sat in silence, wearing dumbstruck expressions. "But what happened to Richard?" Rosie said at last.

Rory reached over and squeezed Rosie's free hand. "David is taking him to Dover. He'll force Richard to sign a commission on a merchant ship. I told David to seek out Gustav Bellerose, the merchant captain with whom my brother, Quinn, used to sail. Gustav will push him hard. He rewards those who are honest and hardworking, but cross him, and his wrath is swift and severe. If Richard survives the voyage, he'll be taken as far as Venice, which will ensure his silence, at least for a good while."

"But he still could return," Mary gasped.

Rory nodded. "He certainly could, but he may also decide to remain in Venice. With the current unrest among the noble families, the region is ripe for an opportunistic swindler. He could thrive there."

Alex snorted. "Which is more than he would have done here had we not intervened. He never would have found a merchant willing to touch the royal treasure, and so he never could have profited from his crime. What's more, when you consider how many people were involved in his plan, I do not doubt the king will learn the name Richard Ash the very moment he realizes he's been robbed."

Rory nodded. "We may have saved his neck in the end."

"I wish ye hadn't," Rosie blurted, dabbing at the tears flowing freely down her cheeks. "I wish ye'd let that Nick fellow slit his throat."

"Rosie," Alex exclaimed, surprised by her maid's blood lust.

"What? 'Tis the truth!"

Rory reached over and patted Rosie's leg. "One day, I've no doubt someone with looser morals than Scotland's agents will slay Richard. But yer lady is no killer, nor am I."

Mary straightened in her seat and squeezed Alex's hand. "We are Christian women, first and foremost. Blood should not be spilled. But I do not understand why ye must leave. Luthmore will stand against anyone who threatens ye."

Alex scooted to the edge of her seat and turned to face her cousin. "Luthmore did not agree to my actions. I have been thieving and secreting messages that many would have killed to read, putting myself in dangerous situation after dangerous situation. I must answer for my actions, not Luthmore. Despite our hope that he will not return to England, vengeance alone may bring him back."

Rory nodded. "If he returns, he will do so with the name Lady Alexandria MacKenzie on his lips, but he cannot make anyone believe him if by all accounts she took to her sickbed during the heist and died soon after."

Alex took a deep breath. "There is no other way. If I flee, then I will look guilty. If I remain, then it is only my word against Richard's—the word of a Scotswoman."

"Who else can know the truth?" Mary asked, her voice barely above a whisper.

Alex turned to her and took her hands. "Only William and Michael, and, of course Abbot Matthew. If ye remember in his letter he promised to journey here in thirty days' time. That is only a few days away. He will be able to help us make arrangements."

"Ye mean, he'll be able to help us plan yer funeral," Rosie huffed.

"I'm afraid so, Rosie," Alex said softly.

"'Tis too much to bear," Mary cried. "How will the clan survive without its lady?"

Alex leaned closer and cupped Mary's cheeks, but her cousin's eyes remained downcast. "Look at me," Alex said softly. "Our clan will thrive as it always has because of ye, Mary. Ye are now Lady of Luthmore."

# Chapter Twenty-One

Alex pulled the tapestry away from her casement just enough to peer down into the garden below where Mary sat on the stone bench, her elegant back straight and long. She was a picture of gentility and grace. Adam sat beside her, but only as close as propriety truly allowed. Alex held her breath as she watched Adam lean across the bench to whisper in Mary's ear. Soft pink highlighted her cousin's cheeks. Then Adam sat back and looked at her with gentle expectancy. Mary's blush deepened but she turned, shifting her body toward Adam before she nodded. A nervous smile tugged at Adam's lips. His hand rested on his thigh, then shifted to grab the bench, then his thigh once more. Finally, he clasped his hands together and leaned forward. Mary slowly did the same. Both sets of eyes closed and lips touched, tentatively at first, a whispered caress, then deeper, more tenderly. Moments later they pulled away, each to their respective sides of the bench.

Alex released a wistful breath before turning away from the window. She had just witnessed Mary and Adam's first kiss—perhaps Mary's first kiss ever. Then she thought about her first kiss with Rory. She had grabbed him, boldly pressing her lips to his.

"How different I am from Mary," she said, joining Michael who sat beside the hearth, staring pensively into the small fire. "She possesses what some might argue are my greatest strengths and none of my flaws. She is the better lady to watch over Luthmore."

Michael shook his head, still watching the flames. "Neither of ye is better or worse than the other, just different."

Alex arched a brow at him. "Yer sentiment over me leaving is making a liar out of ye."

Michael sat up straight in his seat and reached across the divide between their chairs and covered her hand with his. "If I could take back every rebuke, every scolding word I would."

Her throat thickened with tears. "Stop all that. Ye're going to make me cry again. And I spent all morning in tears comforting William. Ye ken I do not wish to go, but ye now know my deeds." She swiped a hand at her tears. "And I would not undo what has been done, not even if I could," she said resolutely. "I have been proud to take up Scotland's sword."

Michael's white brows drew together, his face haggard. "'Tis just that I'll miss ye, lass."

Her heart twisted harder, squeezing out her tears. "Me too, old friend. But remember, we do not part ways forever. When 'tis safe, ye can journey to wherever I end up, and until that time, ye'll be so busy instructing Mary in her duties as lady of the keep, ye won't even notice my absence."

"Ye're wrong there," Michael said, a sad smile lifting his frown. "Mary will need little instruction."

A soft laugh interrupted her dripping tears. "I ken," she said, hiccupping. Then she sighed. "If ye consider the future of our clan with yer head alone, ye'll see that Mary is the better choice. My disregard for convention would likely have been seen as a weakness by other clan leaders, but Mary is goodness and virtue; whereas I am a Scottish rebel with a taste for rugged outlaws."

"'Tis true, my love," Rory said from his seat on her bed. She smiled, meeting his sky-blue eyes.

"Trouble, ye are," he said. "Trouble through and through, but don't worry, Michael. I'll make sure she never changes."

A gentle rapping drew their attention. Rory stood and crossed to stand in front of Alex, then motioned for Rosie to open the door. She opened it just enough to peek into the hallway, then with a gasp, she threw the door wide.

Alex leaned to look past Rory and met crinkled warm, brown eyes. "Abbot Matthew," she exclaimed, jumping to her feet.

He opened his slim arms in preparation for the assault of her hug. "Ye're quite fit for someone who will soon succumb to the pox."

"Nick and Paul told ye everything then?" she said, pulling back to look at his kind face.

The abbot smiled sadly and nodded. "The solution set in place is, I'm afraid and dumbfounded to admit, our best course, especially considering where ye've chosen to place yer heart." The abbot turned and looked sharply at Rory. "I should have known better than to send ye along in the first place." His face softened, and he took hold of their hands. "But given both yer temperaments, yer difficulty following even simple instructions, yer knack for finding danger, and yer overall complete disregard for propriety—I should have known ye'd fall in love at first sight." Then looking at Alex, he said, "In the letter I sent promoting the attributes of Adam, Robert, and Timothy, I should not have cautioned ye against Rory. In doing so, I fear I turned him into forbidden fruit. I should have recommended him above the others, given ye my blessing, and told ye he was a perfect, law-abiding gentleman. Then ye would've stayed clear of him."

Alex smiled at the abbot, then gazed up into Rory's deep-set, heavily lashed eyes. A rakish smile curved his full lips. His black hair fell in careless waves to his broad, thickly muscled shoulders. Keeping his promise to her, the Mackenzie plaid slashed across his bare chest and bunched dangerously low at his waist. He continued to wear his tall, black leather boots. "Honestly, Abbot," she said, never taking her eyes from Rory's. "Do ye think I would have believed ye if ye had?"

The abbot chuckled. "Never."

"With all due respect, Abbot," Rosie chimed in, "'tis too late for all that, anyway."

"Which brings us back to the real matter at hand," Michael said, his sensible reminder drawing everyone's gaze.

"Right ye both are," Abbot Matthew said. Then he cleared his throat and looked at Alex. "The day grows old. We still have yer death to feign and yer funeral to plan."

Alex pressed her lips together in a grim line.

"Well, those aren't phrases ye hear every day," Rosie said, swiping at the tears wetting her pink cheeks.

The abbot crossed the room and put a comforting arm around Rosie's shoulders. "True," he said. "But then 'tis not every day someone robs the king's palace."

Feeling a renewed sense of pride, Alex lifted her chin and locked eyes with the abbot. "*Alba gu bràth*."

# Chapter Twenty-Two

Rory left the keep in the dead of night and made his way on foot to the base of Torna Doon where Michael had tethered a horse for him to ride into Luthmore at first light. He walked the horse in circles to make good his pretense of having traveled through the night, returning for the first time to the castle—at least as far as the rest of the clan was concerned. Having spent the past three days concealed within Alex's chambers, it was, indeed, his first time entering the courtyard. Straightaway, he was struck by the stillness. Sunrise usually sparked a whirl of activity, castle servants going about their morning duties, children playing, warriors readying to train. But the usual din was silenced in the wake of the news Rory knew they would have already received; their lady's health was failing. The grim weather mirrored the apprehension and sadness on the unsmiling faces that looked up to note his return. Gloomy clouds hung heavy with rain that fell in big, cool droplets. No sooner had his booted foot hit the sodden earth when a broad-shouldered man ducked beneath the stable doors.

"Rory," Gavin called before starting across the courtyard with Adam falling in line beside him. Both men appeared weary, their expressions as joyless as their surroundings.

Feigning a look of confusion, Rory's brows came together while he hastened to meet them. "What is it?" Rory said. Then he gestured to the encompassing misery. "What has happened?"

"Alex is ill, gravely so," Gavin said.

Rory raised his brows in a moment of forced surprise an instant before he turned on his heel and headed toward the keep.

"Where are you going?" Adam called after him.

"To the keep. I must see her," he called over his shoulder.

"She will not see you," Adam shouted.

Rory froze, then turned back around. "What do ye mean?"

Adam lifted his shoulders in a helpless gesture. "No one has been permitted to see her. Only my Mary—I mean to say—only Lady Mary and Rosie have been permitted into her chamber. They've hardly left her side since ye left."

"That was the case until two days ago," Gavin corrected. "But now, Michael and William have been called to her side." Gavin's voice cracked. "She's taken a turn for the worse. They do not think she is long for this world."

Rory put a hand on Gavin's shoulder. "Let us out of this rain," he said, steering the men toward the kitchens.

Stepping through the archway, he heard soft sobs combined with the din of chopping and pots clanging. Rory's heart broke when he saw Jean's puffy eyes and trembling lips.

"I can't even bring her a tray like I used to when she was just a sweet, wee lass," she cried while adding chunks of meat to broth nigh brimming out of a bread bowl. "They make me leave it outside her door." Her sobs continued as she lifted the tray in her trembling hands, the broth sloshing over the crusted edges. "They say 'tis a pox."

Rory's stomach twisted with guilt. More than anything, he wanted to bring Alex's kinfolk relief. He wanted to shout at the top of his lungs that their lady was still as vibrant, bold and brave as ever. But then flashes of memory from the Berwick massacre stole his breath. Mass graves filled with the bodies of innocents: men, women, and children. King Edward's heart held no mercy. If he knew Alex had a hand in robbing him, the might of his hammer would demolish Luthmore castle. Unbidden, the images of the villagers in the courtyard, slowly milling about, fretting and grieving over their lady's health were suddenly slain, their bodies broken and strewn across the courtyard. Rory shook the images from his mind. That was exactly what he and Alex were trying to prevent with her feigned demise. Now, if Richard Ash were to return to England and gain Edward's ear and force an inquiry—Edward would learn that the Lady of Luthmore had taken ill before the heist occurred and died from her illness.

Rory opened his arms to Jean. She turned her plump face into his chest and sobbed out her grief. He held his silence, steeling his heart against her sorrow and that of the servants crying soft tears around him. Their lives would be spared, and, in time, their broken hearts would heal.

Very soon it would all be over. He knew when night arrived, Alex would bid goodbye to her family.

ALEX CHOKED BACK HER tears. "I love ye, Will." She swiped at the tears streaming down her brother's freckled face. "Look after Mary for me and keep doing the rounds with her." His sobs tested her resolve. She took a deep breath. "Hush now, sweetling," she crooned. Then she cupped his cheeks. "Look at me, Will MacKenzie. I'm not really dead."

Will nodded and buried his face in her neck. "I ken," he cried. "I just love ye 'tis all. And I'm going to miss ye."

She took a deep breath, reminding herself this was not goodbye forever. Then she reminded Will, "When 'tis safe, ye and Michael will come and visit me. All right?"

Wiping his sleeve across his nose, he nodded. "All right." Then a smile suddenly stretched his face wide. "I've never left Luthmore before."

She chuckled and ruffled his hair. "Ye see, 'tis the makings of a fine adventure." Wiping his nose again, he kissed Alex once more, then crossed the room to stand by Rosie.

"Take care of him," Alex said to Rosie.

Michael stepped forward. "I knew ye weren't just going to visit Abbot Matthew. Although of all the foolhardy things I imagined, what ye really were doing—being part of a secret rebel movement—was not one of them."

She smiled. "This is when ye soften the sting of yer words by saying ye wouldn't have me any other way."

A sad smile crinkled his eyes. "But ye're very much mistaken because I would rather have ye here. Still, I am proud of ye, and yer father and mother would be proud of ye, and Robin for that matter. And I suppose Scotland needs every brave soul she can find—even if that brave soul is ye."

The door opened just a crack and the abbot squeezed into the room. "I've given the bad news to Father John, and he agreed to lay yer body to rest in hallowed ground rather than yer family's tomb, to prevent the spreading of the pox." He crossed to where Alex stood and clasped her hands. "'Tis time, my child. Soon Father John will ring the bell, and Gavin will come for the coffin." He turned then and looked at Michael. "Did ye weigh it down?" he asked.

"We did," Michael confirmed. "And nailed it shut."

The abbot nodded and turned to Alex. "We must be on our way. Rory will have made his excuses by now and will meet us on top of Torna Doon. I shall take ye that far before I return to assist Father John with yer funeral."

She nodded, tears stinging her eyes. "I am nearly ready to go." She turned to Mary and pulled her cousin into a fierce hug. "Give our people every comfort, especially Helen. Tell her I died peacefully." Then she pulled away just enough to remove her necklace. "This is yers now," she said, placing the chain Rory had mended over Mary's head.

Eyes wide, Mary clasped the trinity knot. "But yer mother gave ye this."

Alex wiped the tear she felt course down her cheek. "My mother gave it to me so that I would remember that the well-being of the people comes first. Remember her words, Mary, but also remember mine—yer life matters too. Make yerself happy." Then she stepped away. "I love ye all," she said while she swept her cloak around her shoulders. Then, grabbing the satchel she'd packed, she lifted the trap door. The abbot handed her a torch. She took it and looked at her family. "This is not goodbye," she said once more, her chin quivering before she began her descent—taking the first steps toward her new life.

# Chapter Twenty-Three

Rory stood at the top of Torna Doon, waiting, watching. The August sky would not truly blacken until closer to the midnight hour, lengthening the purple glow of twilight. When he first glimpsed her shadowy form, he hurried forward and swept her into his arms and kissed her with all his love, all his longing. He wanted to soothe away her pain with promises of happiness together.

He pulled away and cupped her cheeks, staring deep into her eyes. "I love ye, Alex. I will always love ye."

The abbot chimed in behind them. "Rory, ye ken they'll be no more women or reckless chances now. 'Tis the end of the road for ye."

Rory smiled, his eyes never leaving hers. "Nay," he whispered, stroking her cheek. "'Tis only the beginning." Then he fell to his knees. "Be my wife."

Laughing, she bent at the waist and threw her arms around his neck. "Ye know I will."

Smiling so wide his face hurt, Rory stood and wrapped his arm around her waist, presenting himself and Alex to the abbot.

"Ye heard her, Abbot. Say the vows before she changes her mind."

The abbot chuckled, shaking his head. "I've told ye before, Rory, I'm not a priest. I cannot marry ye properly, although I can give ye a blessing. Join hands."

Rory turned to face Alex. He clasped her hands, turning them over. His thumbs stroked her calloused palms. Then he bent his head and kissed her.

"Ahem," the abbot said.

Rory stood straight and smiled, meeting Alex's adoring gaze. "I love ye," she whispered and rose up on her tiptoes, kissing him again.

"Ahem," the abbot repeated.

"Sorry, Abbot," Alex said, smiling.

"Shall I begin?"

Rory nodded, resisting the need to crush Alex to his chest and kiss her until her legs gave way.

"Never forget how ye first met," the abbot said, his voice rich with solemnity, but then he shifted his body to the side and winked at Alex. "In yer case, this should be easily done." Clearing his throat, he resumed his reverent posture. "Hold fast to the wonder now in yer hearts and bring that wonder to every word shared and every deed done, however small or big. Do this and yer love shall flourish. For God is love, and He resides in both of ye, binding ye to one another." He stepped back and bowed his head. "I humbly bless this union in His name."

Alex jumped up, wrapping her arms around his neck and kissing him with all her might.

"Now, when ye make it to Colonsay, be sure to have yer marriage solemnized by a priest. And remember, ye can't consummate this union until ye do," the abbot warned.

Rory looked at Alex who looked back with eyes wide. He put her down. Then rubbing the back of his neck, he turned to the abbot. "Well, ye see, Abbott—"

"Nay," Abbot Matthew interrupted, throwing his hand up. "Stop right there. I can't hear confession, and I would rather not know."

Alex stepped forward and pressed a kiss to his cheek. "I'll miss seeing ye as often as I do."

The abbot smiled. "I will miss ye too, my child, and ye, Rory. But before ye go, there is one last thing I must say. Ye have both suffered enough to know the sanctity and fleetingness of life. And ye have both done more than yer share for the cause. Scotland thanks ye. The one thing I ask is that ye both retire yer masks." He reached for Rory's hand and then for Alex's and brought them together, placing his own hands on top of theirs in blessing. "Quiet yer restless souls and let go the cause. Others will pick up where ye've left off."

Rory nodded and gave a shrug. "One more Saint has been unmasked—indirectly at least," he said, winking at Alex.

After bidding the abbot farewell, Alex and Rory mounted their horses and rode out of MacKenzie territory. "We head west then to Colonsay?" she asked.

Rory nodded. "The last time I saw Jack, that is where he was heading. 'Tis where my Father's people hail from. But remember my vow; I care not where we go, just take me with ye."

She smiled. "Colonsay it is. We will join the rest of the Saints. 'Tis too late for me to ride with ye and yer brothers, but at least I will be able to meet them all."

"Jack, my oldest brother should be there, and Ian too."

"Which one is Ian?"

"Ian is the youngest, although he's as big as an ox. His size can be intimidating at first, but ye'll find he's as soft and mild as a lamb until provoked, then...well..."

"Well...what?"

"He has a fierce temper to match his red hair, just like my sister, Rose."

"Will Rose be at Colonsay?"

"Aye. She will."

"Don't ye have another brother? I remember the Saints had five riders."

"Aye, Quinn, but I do not know if he has made it yet to the Isle."

Alex mentally tallied the MacVie brothers. "And Alec is in London makes five." She thought of Rory's older brother with his beautiful stony face and hard eyes. "I pray Alec's soul finds peace."

Rory nodded. "That has always been our hope, too. Who can know—mayhap one day, his heart will feel light, and he will join us all on Colonsay."

Alex smiled at the idea. "How long will the journey take?"

"My guess is we could be there by the week's end if we rode hard." He cleared his throat and looked at her sidelong. "But we needn't rush."

"What did ye have in mind?"

"The Harborage is a fine place for a couple of Scotland's rebels to pass some time."

Leaning out of her saddle, she wrapped her arms around his neck. "Ye're a rogue and a rebel."

"Aye," he whispered and kissed her slowly, passionately. "And ye're my perfect match."

Epilogue

One year later at Luthmore

Michael took a sip of ale, then set his tankard down on his writing table and eased into his chair. His bones ached in protest. How he longed to lie down after several long days of celebration, but he wanted to write his letter while the memories were still fresh. He spread out a fresh piece of parchment, then dipped his quill into the ink pot...

*My Dear Abbot,*

*I hope to somehow convey to ye in writing the joy that right now fills my heart. Sir Adam Lennox married Lady Mary today. I wish you had been able to witness the elegance and solemnity of their wedding. The chapel and courtyard were nigh bursting with villagers. Our kin even gathered on the bridge and surrounded Luthmore's outer wall. The entire clan came to honor and celebrate the new Lord and Lady of Luthmore Castle. Spirits and hopes are high. I am confident Clan MacKenzie will prosper under the compassionate and sensible leadership of Adam and Mary.*

*Father Timothy performed the ceremony with such richness and devotion of spirit. Blessings rain down upon us, for he has agreed to take over the chapel here when Father John retires.*

*Ye will also be happy to know that Sir Robert is also doing well.*

Michael chuckled, then wrote, *Very well, in fact.*

He sat back and took a long gulp of ale. During the wedding, Robert had been missing from his usual spot at the high dais. Instead, he had joined the stable master at one of the trestle tables and, at his side, avidly listening to his every word, was Cara, the beautiful and clearly besotted stable master's daughter.

Michael took up his quill. *I do not think it will be long until Father Timothy has another wedding to perform.*

He laughed out loud as he imagined Robert waiting at the altar astride his prize stallion while the bride trotted down the aisle on a dappled gray mare.

*In other news, William has grown a hand taller and has begun his squire training. Helen is again with child. Corc, bless him, spends every evening with the healer, Morag. We all suspect a romance is brewing there.*

*As for me, with a Lady of Luthmore who wears shoes, I have found time for a little leisure. With that in mind, I hope this letter is the first of many to come. We all look forward to yer next visit to Luthmore.*

*-M*

*P.S. I know you will see this letter to its rightful owner.*

The End

# ALEC: A SCOTTISH OUTLAW

"...Alec is definitely one of the best historical romance novels out there, and a worthy entry in The Scottish Outlaws series." ~ InD'Tale Magazine.

Read Alec and Joanie's story next.
*An excerpt from Alec: A Scottish Outlaw*
*London, England*
*1302*

JOANIE PICARD SWEPT the silk robe from her mistress's shoulders. Diana Faintree, a famed London beauty and singer, dressed in rich fabrics and vibrant hues, but she was as common as Joanie — both born to poverty, both fighting each day to survive.

Frowning, Joanie lifted Diana's arm and inspected the red, horizontal stripes marring the fine skin below her shoulder — thick, evenly spaced markings left behind like a cruel keepsake from their master's biting fingers.

"Leave them for now," Diana said, keeping her eyes averted. "The morning grows old, like me, and we've still much to do."

Joanie nodded and reached for the pumice stone. She ran her thumb across the abrasive, porous surface and winced. She loathed what would happen next. Glancing at Diana's weary face, she couldn't help but suggest, "Where it isn't bruised, your skin is already so soft. Why don't we skip the stone?"

"You already know my answer," Diana said, her lips curving in a soft smile. "But I love you for trying. Go on," she said, the last words at a whisper.

Joanie took a deep breath. Starting at Diana's toes and working her way up her long leg, she set to work scouring Diana's skin with the stone in small, circular motions.

"You're too gentle," Diana said, gritting her teeth.

Joanie looked up at her. "You are not well. I do not wish to hurt you."

A forced smile stretched Diana's lips wide. "I'm fine. You worry too much." She shifted her gaze away from Joanie's. "Do it right."

Joanie looked longingly at the window and imagined throwing back the shutters and hurling the hateful stone beyond the palace walls. She tightened her grip around it. If only she could crush it to dust, but then her fingers fell slack, the stone neither soaring through the air nor crumbling to the floor. It filled her palm, and it was just as well — Diana would only procure another for her routine ablutions. For nearly five years, Joanie had served as Diana's maid, and in all that time, they had never skipped her weekly rigorous beauty treatments — despite any new bruises received at the hands of their master or her failing health. Pressing her lips together in a grim line, Joanie gripped Diana's thigh and continued scrubbing until her skin shone red.

"Have the others faded?" Diana asked when Joanie scooted on her knees around to Diana's backside. Angry bruises in varying shades of red, brown, and yellow marred her back, buttock, and thighs.

"A little," Joanie said, setting the stone aside. She reached into a basket of tins and pouches filled with various creams, ointments and powders. She took up the comfrey ointment. She scooped a great dollop of the greasy balm, then dotted it over Diana's bruises before gently rubbing the soothing ointment into her skin.

"Geoffrey was in a particularly foul mood last night," Diana murmured.

Joanie didn't respond. When was the master not in a foul mood?

"Look at me," Diana entreated her.

Joanie did as she was bidden.

"Your interference must stop. He was vexed with me, not you. He never would have touched you had you not stepped in front of me."

Joanie lowered her gaze and continued applying the balm. "You cannot ask me to stand idly by while he beats you." Then she stopped rubbing and looked up, locking eyes with her mistress once more. "I will not do that," she avowed through gritted teeth.

"Joanie—" Diana began, but then a deep, wet cough stole her words and her breath. Her whole body jerked as if under attack from the inside out. Joanie jumped to her feet and wrapped her arms around Diana to support her. When at last the coughing ceased and Diana caught her breath, she wiped at her eyes and smiled weakly at Joanie. "Thank you," she rasped. Then she slowly reached out a trembling hand toward the hem of Joanie's tunic. "How do your gifts from our master fare?"

Diana's weakened state broke Joanie's heart. Shaking her head, she implored, "Do not worry for me. Mine always heal quickly." Then she scooped more salve and spread it over the fresh fingerprints on Diana's arm. "You must save your strength. I'm nearly finished, then you can get into the bath." Joanie glanced at the tub in front of the hearth. Steam curled in ghostly ribbons from the oily surface.

"It will do me good. I know it will," Diana said. Then she smiled at Joanie. "I see your worry. It is etched on your dear face, visible even beneath the grime you refuse to let me help scrub away. This cough will pass."

Joanie frowned. "I'm only permitted to bathe once a fortnight. I do not fancy being clean enough to attract the master's fury." She looked away before continuing in a gentle voice. "The cough is persisting this time."

"I know," Diana said.

The truth hung in the air between them for a moment like an ominous cloud, but Diana chased the storm away with her bright voice. "Anyway, you've always managed to cure me in the past."

Joanie scanned Diana's body. Unlike Joanie, who was shorter and slimly built, Diana had always enjoyed lush, full curves that drove men wild. But her cough had worsened over the last fortnight, and her body had begun to waste away. Joanie fought to keep her concern from showing. "The next time Simon checks in on us, I am going to have him bring up another meal for you."

Diana shook her head. "I am still full after breaking our fast. I couldn't possibly eat again so soon."

"You will if you want to be stronger." Joanie wrapped her arm around Diana's waist. "Let me help you into the bath."

"Wait," Diana said.

Joanie stood still and looked at her expectantly.

"Could I have a mirror?"

Nodding, Joanie reached for the small, gilded compact on Diana's bedside table and gave it to her. Diana held the glass up, scrutinizing her features. She pulled at the skin beneath her eyes and the soft lines framing her mouth. "I'm a disgrace."

Joanie glanced up from the beauty mask she was mixing. "You are the most beautiful woman in London."

Diana's expression softened. "And you are forever my champion, even when I battle myself." Then she turned back and continued studying her own reflection. "I was the most beautiful woman in London. But age is robbing me of the title all too soon. That is what happens when you turn thirty."

"You are not yet thirty."

"No, but I am eight and twenty." Diana frowned again at what she saw in the mirror. "I may as well be a hundred." With a sigh, she set the compact down. "At nineteen, Joanie, you can hardly understand." Then she slid the robe from her shoulders and continued in a brighter voice. "Have you mixed the porridge mask?"

Joanie nodded, relieved for the change in subject. "Let's get you into the tub first." She helped Diana step into the steamy water. Joanie had poured liberal amounts of chamomile and lavender oils into the bath to soothe Diana's bruises, and the heady scents wafted off the surface as the water rose to make room for her battle-wearied body. Diana groaned when she eased back. Joanie smiled, realizing by the contented look on Diana's face that she voiced her pleasure rather than discomfort. Picking up the clay dish filled with a mixture of roughly cut oats and heavy cream, she smoothed a thick layer onto Diana's upturned face.

"What will I do when my looks finally go, Joanie? Geoffrey will turn me out."

Flashes of the master's hulking fists and cruel eyes raced through Joanie's mind, chasing her smile away. "Would that really be so awful?"

Diana opened her eyes and gave Joanie a hard look. "There are worse pains than fist or lash. Hunger. Cold. They are the real demons." Her face softened. "I know you have suffered greatly at the hands of your masters and your father before he sold you. But Joanie..." Diana shifted her gaze but not before Joanie saw the sudden sheen of unshed tears in her eyes. "You have never known true hunger or cold. Don't ever fool yourself into thinking you'd be better off somewhere else." Diana turned back to look at her. Her tears were gone, and her eyes shone clear and strong. "Our master is rich." She lifted a dripping hand from the water and made a sweeping gesture. "Look at this room, at the warm bed we share and in the king's palace, no less. We are the lucky ones, Joanie. Out there, the streets are full of people a breath away from death who would withstand any number of abuses to have what we possess."

Joanie shifted her gaze away from Diana's stubborn resolve wondering whether her friend was right. Were they, indeed, better off with the master? More than once, she had asked Diana to run away with her, but she had always refused and warned Joanie not to dream beyond survival. But Joanie couldn't help wondering — was it really a choice between beatings and abuse or starvation and freezing? Couldn't there be another life for them — one without the constant threat of pain or death? She dipped her finger into a pot of honey and willow oil and worked the mixture into her hands before gently weaving her fingers through Diana's wet hair.

Her mistress sighed as her elbows came up on the sides of the tub. "That feels so good. I've had such a headache."

"You should have told me sooner," Joanie scolded. Then she cupped her hand and closed her eyes, imagining a ball of light at rest in her palm. Curving her palm over Diana's forehead, she closed her eyes and took deep, slow breaths and imagined heat radiated from the light in her hand, surrounding Diana's pain. She stayed there for a long while, confronting the darkness with her healing touch.

Diana sighed. "You're an angel."

Joanie opened her eyes. "You don't believe in angels."

Diana smiled. "For the moment I do."

"Then the pain is gone. Good," Joanie said, happy to have alleviated at least a little of Diana's suffering. She wrapped her fingers around the handle of a small copper pot and dipped it in the bath water to rinse Diana's hair. But a sharp rapping on the door startled her, and she dropped the handle, losing the pot beneath the surface. Jumping to her feet, she came around the screen that shielded her mistress, just as a barrel-chested man of great height with thinning brown hair, a neatly trimmed beard, and a red nose from too much ale walked into the room.

Joanie expelled the breath she'd been holding. "Thank God it's you, Simon."

Simon was their master's manservant. To most people, he was gruff and hard — full of bite, but beneath his coarse surface, hid a gentleness only shown to Diana and thus to Joanie by default.

He motioned toward the screen and mouthed the words, how is she?

Lips pressed into a thin line, Joanie only shook her head in answer.

"Damn it," Simon cursed.

Straightaway, Joanie's heart started to pound. "What is it?" she whispered. Then she heard the water slosh and knew Diana had sat up.

"Is that Simon? Is something wrong?"

His powerful shoulders sagged. Sad eyes met Joanie's. "Geoffrey wants you in the hall tonight," he said loud enough for Diana to hear.

Joanie's eyes widened. "But tonight is Anabel's night to entertain."

Simon put his hand up, silencing her protest. "She doesn't have to perform, but he insists she attend the evening meal and stay for the entertainment following."

Water sloshed again. Joanie hurried around the screen.

"I must get out," Diana said, struggling to stand. "My hair will never dry in time. And my gown still needs freshening. Joanie, what will I — "

Joanie's chest tightened at the sound of Diana's sudden cough, which racked her shoulders. She white-knuckled the sides of the tub to keep her face out the water. Joanie dropped to her knees and wrapped her arms around Diana, supporting her. Wet hacking subsided into strangled wheezing and finally gasps for air. When, at last, the cough ran its course, Diana turned her face up to look at Joanie. Joanie's heart ached at the sight of her red, tear-streaked face and wide, terrified green eyes. She trembled in Joanie's arms. "Let's get you dry," Joanie said, her voice soothing. She helped Diana step from the tub, then dried her off and swept her robe around her shoulders.

"She is decent," Joanie called. "I need your help, Simon."

Simon appeared an instant later, his face drained of color. He scooped Diana into his arms.

"Simon's got you." Joanie heard him whisper.

Joanie hurried around the screen and rushed to the bed, grabbing pillows and blankets, which she then arranged near the hearth. "Lay her down and fan her hair out so it dries," she told him. Then she hurried to the table and seized a small pouch of mustard powder from a basket, which she quickly mixed with flour, warm water from the bath, and vinegar. Then she knelt beside Diana.

"Make sure she is ready," Simon said to Joanie.

She nodded and carried on mixing the mustard paste while she watched Simon gently stroke Diana's cheek with the back of his fingers. Then he stood and strode from the room.

Joanie gave the thick paste a final stir. Then she opened Diana's robe, exposing her chest.

"No," her mistress said, waving her away. "I will stink. Just lay your hands on me. Your touch alone has healed me before."

Joanie shook her head. "I promise it will wash away, and lavender oil will hide the smell. It will hopefully stave off another attack for some time, allowing you to regain your strength."

Diana closed her eyes. "Fine, but just a thin layer. Then you must ready my face."

Joanie thickly coated her chest with the foul-smelling mixture, despite her protests. Then she set to work combining a fine white powder with vinegar and egg white. Using a bristly brush, she made sweeping strokes across Diana's mottled complexion, until it gleamed white. Then she dabbed soft pink rouge on the apples of both her cheeks. Taking a step back, she scrutinized Diana's appearance.

Her brows were plucked to thin, pale crescent moons. Her hair cascaded across the floor in thick waves and shone almost white, it was so blond. She did not require onion skins or lemon juice to lighten the color, unlike so many of the women at court, whose dull hair looked more orange than blond as a result of their efforts. Everything about Diana was naturally built to seduce, from her curvy figure to the throaty tone of her voice. And when she sang, men stopped and stared with hungry eyes. Joanie chewed her lip as she impatiently waited for her mistress's hair to dry.

Simon returned a few hours later. "That will have to do," he said, his voice strained. "The hour for supper is almost here."

He gently helped Diana to her feet and wrapped his arm around her waist.

"No," she said, not unkindly. "I can manage."

Tears stung Joanie's eyes as she watched her mistress gracefully cross the room to sit at her table where a gilded mirror reflected her ethereal beauty. Knowing the pain she must have felt tore at Joanie's heart, although Diana let none of it show.

Joanie crossed the room and took hold of Diana's comb and pulled her long bangs back to lengthen her brow. When her hair was pinned in place, she arranged the sides so that golden waves spilled over Diana's shoulders past her waist. Then she helped her dress.

"Will Geoffrey approve?" Diana asked nervously, smoothing her hands over the intricately embroidered bodice of her pale green tunic.

Joanie doubted anyone could ever fully meet with the master's approval. Still, Diana's beauty was unmatched regardless of the passing of time. "You look stunning. Mind you do not overdo it. Hold your tongue so that you do not strain your voice. Remember, you have to perform tomorrow night."

Diana nodded. "I will remember. I am hoping to get away as soon as I can."

Simon filled the doorway with his large frame. "It is time."

Diana stood and kissed Joanie on the cheek before she crossed the room and left on Simon's arm.

Joanie stared at the closed door for a moment. Then she numbly turned and stiffly sat in Diana's seat and looked at her own reflection in the mirror. Her greasy black hair hung limply past her shoulders. Her brown eyes looked back at her, dull, void of joy and life. As ever, her face was hidden beneath a layer of dirt and grime. Her master didn't allow her a bath of her own. None of the ointments, oils, or perfumes on the table were for her use. She wore the same worn, tattered tunic every day. Once a fortnight, she was permitted to wash herself and her clothing in Diana's used bath water. Not for her own benefit or health, but only so that the master didn't have to smell her. Geoffrey Mercer's cruel, twisted smiled came to the fore of her mind. Unlike Diana, she at least did not have to face him every day. Diana went to his room to perform her duties as leman. But whenever he did enter their room, it always meant the worst. The sound of his footfalls and that of his guard, who followed him everywhere, would echo through the stone corridor like thunder. A shiver shot up Joanie's spine just thinking about the din of their master's approach. She closed her eyes. Her heart pounded. Her breaths came short.

"Help us," she whispered to no one, for who would hear the pleas of someone as insignificant as she?

Joanie whirled away from the sad creature she saw in the mirror, stood up and started to clean the room. She would keep moving, keep doing, despite her fatigue. She couldn't stop. If she did, she would be forced to face the truth about Diana who was her one light in the dark. Her beloved mistress's health had been failing for months, but she had managed with Joanie's help. Still, the past fortnight had taken its toll.

"No," she said out loud and fought back her tears.

After all, Diana continued to fight. She carried on, bravely surviving, and so would Joanie. That is what life had always been. It was what life would always be — a desperate fight for survival.

*FRIGID GUST OF WINTER'S chill strikes Alec's face while he hovers in the night air far above the city of London. Orange torch fire flickers like stars across the shadowy cityscape. Silence engulfs him, soothes him. He is cold and alone, but his mind is all his own, not burdened by other's emotions or visions of tragedies yet to come. He is out of reach, flying above the human pain revealed to his seer's eyes.*

*But then he feels a tug from below.*

*"No," he says, his voice flat.*

*He turns onto his back and stares up at stars, distant guardians, but of whom or what? He once believed they were angels, but he stopped believing in angels long ago. Too many people suffered needlessly for angels to be real. He covers his face with his hands. Again, he feels a pull in his heart, a soul pleading for his. His hands fall away. Large snowflakes cascade and dance, whirling in swirling circles from a now starless sky. He sighs and spreads his arms wide, like a bird, and drifts down. The vague city shapes become defined — shacks, warehouses, churches, fortresses, docks, riverboats, and bridges.*

*Then he sees her.*

*She is standing on a narrow, wrought iron bridge, guarded by two lions, their faces watchful and regal. But those stone sentinels cannot save her, only he can. Her shoulders tensely hug her ears as she pulls the folds of her tattered cloak tighter against the wintry night. Fear and pain coil like writhing snakes around her heart. His long arm extends, reaching down to her, comforting her. Her wide dark eyes brim full of tears. Heartbroken. Hungry. Cold.*

*Her pleas ride upon the whirling snow until they reach his ear in a whisper. "Help us."*

*He descends, swooping down, stopping a breath away from her face. He meets her gaze.*

*"Alec," she whispers, a puff of icy breath leaving her lips.*

Alec MacVie sat up with a start, his thin wool blanket pooling around his hips. His heart pounded in his ears, along with the dizzying accompaniment of another's heartbeat, her heartbeat. He threw back the covers, swung his legs over the side of the bed, and rested his head in his hands. A flash of cold lingering from the wintry dream passed over him, chilling his naked body. Shivering, he wrapped his fingers around the shard of stone, nearly purple in color, which hung from a long, leather strip around his neck. Heat emanated from the stone. He closed his eyes, inviting the warmth to imbue his body. The chill fled, but whoever she was, the poor, heartbroken lass on the bridge, her pain still gripped his soul. Her fear quickened his own pulse. He took a deep, slow breath and willed it all to cease. Slowly, everything drained away, leaving the hollowness inside him to which he had grown accustomed.

He crossed to stand in front of the hearth. Orange embers glowed in the darkness. Closing his eyes, he again saw her pale face and heard his name on her lips. Still staring at smoldering ash, he backed up a few steps and sat in the high-backed chair. The stone shard he wore now felt cool against his skin. He wrapped his fingers around it, wondering about the secrets it held — secrets kept even from his divining gaze.

The stone had come to him by the Abbot Matthew of Haddington Abbey. The Abbot led a secret network of Scottish rebels to which Alec and his brothers belonged. Before setting out on his latest assignment, the abbot had given Alec the shard and told him that it contained a secret he hoped Alec could reveal — a secret of great importance to the cause.

"Somehow, Scotland's fate is tied to this broken shard," the abbot had told him.

For months now, he had pondered the stone, but it had remained quiet, soulless; that is, until three nights ago, when he started dreaming about the lass on the bridge. Suddenly, the stone had allusively revealed itself, warming when her heartbeat accompanied his own. This was the third time he had dreamt of her, and now the third time he had felt the stone's fire. But who was she? And what did it all mean?

He raked both hands through his hair, as he glanced about the room. One thing he knew for certain — the answers were not hiding there in his chamber. He needed to get out. Letting the cool stone fall against his chest, he stood and crossed to his wardrobe and grabbed a pair of hose. He pulled them on, settling the waistband low on his hips. Then he yanked on a black tunic, which he belted at his waist. Within his tall boots, he hid a dagger. And after securing his sword to his back, he swept a thick, black cloak over his shoulders and headed toward the door.

Stepping into the hallway, he shut the door and locked it before setting out down the corridor, which was illuminated by candlelight. At the end of the hallway, he turned onto a landing. His eyes, as always, were drawn straight ahead where a massive shield bore the King of England's coat of arms. The large display served as Alec's daily reminder that he was, indeed, living in King Edward's palace in London — or at least a wealthy English merchant named Randolph Tweed was.

For several months now, Alec had been living under the alias of Randolph Tweed, spying on the English court by order of Abbot Matthew. But in all that time, King Edward had not actually been in residence. He had moved his household to York where he readied his army for war, bringing a six-month truce with Scotland soon to an end. In his absence, he had left his palace in London in the less than capable hands of a man named John Bigge. The keepership was John's according to hereditary laws, but as keeper, he had done little to preserve courtly order. Rather, his salacious appetites had invited all manner of sinners to court. He had even tempted the monks in the adjacent abbey to partake in his unholy revelries. In fact, it was rumors of the monks' debauchery that compelled the abbot to send one of his secret rebels to the palace in the first place, and it was no surprise that he assigned Alec to the task.

Of all the secret rebels in Scotland, Alec was particularly adept as a spy, owing to gifts that had both served and plagued him his entire life. In the simplest of terms, Alec possessed the Sight. He could feel what another person was feeling, and if he laid his hand on someone, he saw into their soul — their fears, pains, sorrows, and desires. When it served him to be charming, no one could resist him. He could sense a person's response to him, guiding his word and deed. They invariably told him exactly what they needed to hear. Lies could never fool him. Detecting deception came as naturally to him as breathing. More than that, he had visions, dreams that revealed need or what loomed in the future — like his dream of the heartbroken lass on the bridge.

When he was not pretending to be someone else, he chose to isolate his thoughts, to buffer and block out the voices. Over the years, he had learned to erect walls around his senses, shielding his heart and mind from the continuous barrage of human emotion. As a result, most thought him cold-hearted ... a hard man. And whether true or not, he did nothing to change their minds. He preferred to keep people at a distance. They were all too human, too quick to distrust and to assume the worst of themselves and others. The inner workings of another's mind were seldom uplifting. Most of the time, it was like walking through a nightmare of despair, and the king's palace was no different. The keeper had amassed a collection of companions with the vilest of hearts, bent only on baseless pleasures.

He knew not the hour as he approached the great hall, but he would be able to judge the time depending on how drunk the revelers were. He closed his eyes, steeling his strength against the assault of emotion as he pulled open the large double doors and walked headlong into the large room. Piercing laughter and battling voices echoed off the vaulted ceilings. Raucous men salivated after dancers who languidly moved among the tables, undulating their hips in layers of sheer silk. Barmaids busily skirted around the dancers, filling greedy fists with large tankards of ale at a speed that meant the night was still young.

He took a step forward just as one of the dancers twirled away from groping hands straight into Alec. Her hands splayed across his chest as she looked up to meet his eyes. Flashes of her life came unbidden to his mind; a little girl loved and treasured, a father lost at sea, a mother with no place to turn, a life torn asunder, a beautiful young woman alone.

"I'm sorry," she said, a sensual smile curving her lips. But then her eyes narrowed on his, and her smiled vanished. She dropped her hands to her sides. "Randolph," she said, surprise and trepidation lacing her voice.

He held her gaze but revealed none of what he'd glimpsed of her. Nor did he acknowledge her distrust of him. The dancers and serving maids were all afraid of him. They had seen his black eyes and cool facade and assumed the worst of him. Rumors abounded of his cruel sexual appetites, although he had never taken any one of them to his bed. Still, he did naught to dispel the rumors as it kept them away. Eyes now wide, the dancer turned and darted away from him.

He cleared her from his thoughts, emptying his heart and mind, choosing numbness over the lust, greed, hunger, and fear, which pulsed through the room and fought to enter him. Only snatches of emotion made it past. But then an ache so soft and pure, cut through the rest, overtaking all his defenses. Pain accompanied by truth rang out, even in its gentleness, above the din of desperation. His eyes fell on a woman he had seen many times before. Her name was Diana. Her flaxen hair trailed the ground where she sat, and her green eyes shone with mirth and delight. She was an actress without equal. Those surrounding her, her many admirers, could never have guessed the pain she was in. Only Alec knew that which even she might not have known herself. She was dying. He could feel the struggle for life in her waning heartbeat, but something or someone was keeping her alive. He looked at the large, detestable man at her side and knew he was not the reason behind her strength.

"Randolph," a voice called out.

Alec turned and locked eyes with the keeper. John's thick black hair curled close to his scalp. He had just celebrated his fortieth year with all the pomp of a true royal despite the humbleness of his birth. He was neither lord nor knight, but he carried himself as though he were king. He raised his tankard as Alec approached. "Randolph, I've not seen you for days." His small, brown eyes darted left then right before he continued in a quiet voice. "Have you any news?"

Alec, of course, knew what John sought. Unbeknownst to anyone, from the very beginning, Alec had been pitting John's companions against one another, mostly merchants and some lesser nobles, inciting conflict among the ranks. Then he revealed the subsequent deceptions and misgivings to John, earning his unquestioned trust. In turn, John's approval protected him from the others, that and his own stony demeanor.

"I've nothing to report," Alec said, his face and voice impassive.

John nodded, then his eyes left Alec's as one of the dancers enticed him with the gentle sway of her hips. The keeper grabbed her. Alec looked away. Hazy drunkenness blurred John's emotions, but he had at least what he thought he wanted — a tankard in one hand and a woman on his lap who was not his wife. Alec resisted the urge to shake his head in disgust as John palmed the dancer's breast. He turned and started to walk away. He had to get out of there.

"Will you not join us?" the keeper called.

Alec glanced back. "I've some business to take care of."

"Some evening you must bring your business here so that we might meet her," the keeper called after him, laughing.

With a cool nod, Alec turned away from John's greed. Ignoring the stares as he passed through the revelers, he stepped out into the courtyard and welcomed the sting of icy wind. The city awaited him, and perhaps this night he would find what kept him in London — the lass from his dreams.

Find your copy of Alec: A Scottish Outlaw at Amazon.com.
Wishing you happy reading and many blessings.
All my best,
Lily Baldwin

Manufactured by Amazon.ca
Bolton, ON

42197233R00141